The

Self-Improvement

Book Club

Murder

by

Todd Wright

OLD WORLD LIBRARY

New York, New York

Library of Congress Cataloging-in-Publication Data

Wright, Todd, 1964-

ISBN-13: 978-1456461355

ISBN-10: 1456461354

For Michelle

"Bookman, check this out. Says here, 'The ego creates separation, and separation creates suffering.' That's pretty profound, don't you think?"

"Does this have anything to do with the case?"

"Well, no, not exactly, but—"

"Then I'm not interested."

Chapter 1

"Morning, Charlie."

"Body's in the living room. Where's Bookman?"

"I called him," Berg said, holding up his cell phone. "No answer." Charlie's eyebrows wrinkled.

"Don't worry," Berg said. "I can handle it."

"I'm sure you can," Charlie said. "But Bookman—"

"I know," Berg said. "We'll just have to make the best of it."

Detective Berg followed Charlie into the crime scene. The carpet was soaked with blood around the feminine body, dressed in a business suit, belled slacks, cuffs turned back. The open collar revealed the mortal wound.

"Shot through the neck," Charlie said.

"Clean wound."

"We haven't found the bullet yet."

"Keep looking," Berg said. "Has she got a name?"

"Sue Ellen Pinkus."

"Pinkus," Berg repeated. It sounded familiar.

"Dad's the big dry cleaners mogul."

Berg nodded, remembering.

A tri-folded sheet of bright yellow paper lay by her outstretched left hand, a handprint in blood across the front of it.

Berg asked, "What's this?"

"Looks like a homemade brochure of some kind," Charlie said. "That's the victim's paw print across the front." Charlie crouched down beside the coffee table to point out a smear of blood across its corner. "See that? After the perp shot her, he must have left in a hurry, leaving the victim with just enough life to reach up for this thing. With a wound like that she wouldn't have lasted long."

"May I?" Berg said, pointing to the brochure.

"Could be prints on it," Charlie said. "Use these." He handed Berg a set of drug store tweezers.

"These regulation?" Berg said.

"They get the job done."

Berg pried open the cover of the brochure, the title of which was "Self-Improvement Book Club." Inside was a black and white photo of a squirrelly, bearded character named Todd Gack. A few titles were listed, an address. The club met every Monday night.

"What do you think?" Charlie said.

"Looks like a pretty interesting book club," Berg said. "I wouldn't mind attending, myself."

"I have a feeling you're going to get your chance tonight," Charlie said. "If you ever find Bookman."

"I'll find him," Berg said. "Who found her?"

"The boyfriend," Charlie said. "He's waiting in

the squad car with Dugan."

"Time of death?"

"Sometime on Saturday."

Charlie went away. Berg looked around. Tasteful decor, cream, beige and pink. Nice stuff, looked expensive. A woman lived here, alone. Not much of a housekeeper: a couple of books on the couch, cluttered shelves, a stack of towels on the stairs waiting to go up—at least they were folded. No sign of a struggle.

Ipod on the shelf, in a Bose sound dock. Berg called over a technician to dust it for prints.

"Wiped clean, eh?" Berg said, when she finished.

"Yep."

Berg took it out and powered it up. It was set to play Stevie Wonder. He put it back in the dock and clicked it on. "I just called...to say...I love you..." He clicked it off again.

Telephone in the kitchen. No answering machine. A stack of *Bits and Pieces* magazines on the counter—never heard of it—the mailing address clipped away, like in a dentist's office. Nothing on the table. Dishes in the sink. Of note in the trash can: a bottle of wine, American label, there was the cork, a butter wrapper, a Lean Cuisine box, glazed chicken with brown rice.

The technician came in to do her dusting.

Folded bills on the counter, varying denominations, loose change on the tile floor. "She seemed to have a total disregard for money," Berg said.

The technician smiled. "I guess."

Berg went out.

On the stoop, he buttoned his overcoat. Berg's hair was slicked back and his suit was expensive, too expensive for his salary, especially now that he was living on his own and making child support payments. But he hadn't been a detective that long. He still felt the need to dress for success.

Berg could see the boyfriend through the windshield of the cruiser. His head was down. As he made his way across the spongy grass, walking stiff-legged so as not to slip down the slight slope, Berg watched Dugan point in his direction and the boyfriend look up and get out of the car. Good looking guy. A little pasty. Collared shirt, sweater, brown corduroy jacket, fleece lining.

"I'm Detective Alec Berg," he said, flashing his badge.

"I, uh..." the man said.

"I know this is difficult," Berg said. "But I have to ask you a few questions."

"We hadn't been going out all that long, you know. I feel bad saying it but we were probably going to go our separate ways pretty soon, except..."

"What's your name?"

"Scott Drake."

"Except for what, Mr. Drake?"

"Well, we work together."

"Office romance," Berg said.

"Yeah," Drake said. "So it was difficult to, you

know..."

"Where?"

"The Human Fund," Drake said. "It's a non-profit organization that puts together adoptions from third-world countries."

"So she was a social worker," Berg said. "Pretty nice neighborhood."

"Oh, she didn't need the money," Drake said. "Her family's pretty well off. She did it because she was a genuinely good person. She wanted to make a difference."

"And you're not into that?"

"We'd been going out for a few months, everything was going well. And then she changed."

"What do you mean?"

"Hard to describe," Drake said. "But I think it had something to do with a book club she'd gotten herself wrapped up in."

"A book club."

"A self-help book club. Guy named Gack runs it. Everybody picks a book and talks about it. You know."

"What was her book?"

"*The Power of Positive Thinking*," Drake said.

"Kind of ironic."

"Gack's was some new age crap I've never heard of."

"Sounds like you're not particularly found of Mr. Gack," Berg observed. "You think they were involved?"

"I had my suspicions," Drake said. "I went with Sue Ellen once to a meeting. Let's just say I didn't feel welcome."

"Did you pick a book?"

"Yeah," Drake said with a smirk. "*He's Just Not That Into You.* It was disqualified."

"That couldn't have been good for the relationship, either," Berg said.

Drake shrugged and stuffed his hands into the pockets of his jacket. "Meets every Monday. Check it out yourself tonight, if you like."

"What brings you here so early on a Monday morning?"

"Oh, Sue Ellen's house is on my way to work."

"So that was your in," Berg said.

"Yeah, that was my in," Drake said. "I'm sorry, I'm just kind of freaked out right now."

"I understand," Berg said. "But I have to ask, where were you this weekend?"

"You don't think..."

"I have to ask."

"No way, man," Drake said. "I was out of town all weekend. I was visiting my folks a state away. I got home last night around eleven. Lot's of people can verify that."

"We just have to check everything out, that's all," Berg said. "So if you can give us your parents' contact information, it'll put our minds at ease." He handed Drake pen and paper.

"'Our'?"

"Sorry," Berg said. "We usually work these cases in twos. And if you could write down what you know about Mr. Gack, that would be helpful too."

Drake got in his car and drove away. Charlie

sidled up to Berg.

"So what do you want us to do when we're finished here?" he asked.

"Take your time with it, Charlie. I'll try to get Bookman down here. When I find him."

* * *

"This Sue Ellen Pinkus is what they call a socialite, Detective Berg. Do you know what that means?" Chief Inspector Farkus stood behind his desk, sleeves rolled up, tie wagging, black face shiny. "It means we have an opportunity this election season. If we find her killer, the boss's re-elected is a lock. You understand what I'm telling you, son?"

"I think I do, yes, sir."

"Where's Bookman?"

Berg shifted from one foot to the other. "He said you fired him."

"Fired him? I didn't fire him."

"Suspended?"

"I just gave him a talking to about his drinking."

Berg cringed. "You did what?"

"Just a little man-to-man, that's all," Chief Farkus said.

"Ah, Jeez," Berg said. "Next thing you're telling me, you told him not to go to Mass every day."

"Well, now that you mention it—"

"Look, boss," Berg said. "You're kind of new to the job so I'm going to give it to you straight. John Bookman is the best detective the city of Plimpton has ever known. He sees things other people don't see. Two things we never discuss

11

with Bookman: alcohol and religion."

"Is that right?" Farkus said, lowering his voice.

"I'm just giving it to you straight, sir."

"Get the hell out of my office."

"Yes, sir."

"And find Bookman!"

* * *

"Bookman? You in there?" Berg knocked again. "Bookman?"

"What do you want?" Bookman shouted through the door.

"The Chief says he didn't fire you?" Berg shouted back. "Come on, Bookman, open the door."

Bookman put his bottle of Old Granddad away, then popped in a mint on his way to the door. There was nothing he could do about the tiny pink veins in his bulbous nose or about the bloodshot of his pale blue hound dog eyes.

As he opened up, he said, "'Let us send forth chosen men to go forthwith to the hut of Peleus' son, Achilles.'"

"What is that?"

Bookman turned his back on Berg and walked the shallow depth of his studio apartment. "It's from *The Iliad*." He sat down in the recliner and turned on the television with the remote.

Berg had been to Bookman's hotplate hovel before. He turned one of the kitchen chairs around and straddled it. "The chief said he didn't fire you."

"No?" Bookman said, feigning disinterest. "Well, something happened."

Something, indeed, had happened to Bookman in that meeting. Chief Farkus had started in on him about his drinking, how it was affecting his work. Tardiness, too many sick days, how it was a poor example for the younger detectives. Bookman had responded that Chief Peterman never had a problem with his work habits, that he focused on the bottom line, cases solved, that no one was better at that than himself and that perhaps it would be in Chief Farkus's best interests to do as his predecessor had done and mind his own business.

These confrontations came along once every few years. The insult would cause Bookman to buckle down for a while but no matter what he did, no matter how hard he tried to withstand temptation, sooner or later the bottle would always take him away again. It was his Achilles heel. Another meeting, another insult, and the pain—the suffering—had gotten progressively worse with each new iteration.

In the meeting with Farkus, Bookman had stood his ground as he always did but the pain that the insult inflicted during that brief exchange became too much to bear. Bookman felt something crack, a burden lift. A slender blade of light shone through and momentary peace pervaded his being.

But Bookman had his role to play and he kept to it, walking out on Farkus, as he always had before in these interventions, sputtering something about quitting the force.

"I don't know what happened, Bookman," Berg

said. "I wasn't there."

Berg, in his two years of apprenticeship studying under the master detective, had seen this scenario before. The first time came just after Berg's promotion. What had seemed a minor slight from another of the senior detectives had sent Bookman running for the bottle, threatening to quit the force. That was right in the middle of the Smog Strangler investigation. Admittedly, Berg was unnerved at first. But his quick reactions and fast learning seemed to endear him to Bookman, who before had seen his young partner as nothing more than a pretty face with nothing much upstairs. After that incident, Bookman swore by Berg, even when he went through a tough time during his divorce. Farkus's predecessor, Peterman, wanted to send Berg back to uniformed duty but Bookman raised enough of a stink that the plan was scrapped.

"Use your powers of deductive reasoning," Bookman said. "You're a detective. You're on your own now. I've taught you everything you need to know." Bookman glanced at Berg from the corner of his eye, then refocused on the TV screen.

"Come on, Bookman," Berg said. "We've got a live one here. We need your help. Sue Ellen Pinkus of the Pinkus family, heiress to the Pinkus Dry Cleaners fortune, was murdered over the weekend."

"What's this got to do with me?"

Berg said, "I talked to the Chief. I gave him a

stern talking to. He made a mistake. He said it won't happen again."

Bookman turned down the volume on the television. "The chief's going to have to come down here himself."

"You know that's not going to happen, Bookman. He hasn't got that kind of time. The man is in way over his head as it is. He needs your help. Look, he said he was sorry. What more do you want?"

"Something happened to me in that office," Bookman said. "I don't know what it was, but it was something."

"Come on, Bookman. This case is just the way you like 'em. Old school. No prints, no DNA. We're going to solve it—if we solve it—the old fashioned way."

Bookman pointed at the TV screen with the remote. "I've been watching the Travel Channel. A special on Florida. I've got plenty of time in, you know. I think I'll retire. I have a sister who lives down in Tampa. Haven't spoken to her in years but you never know."

"Bookman, please," Berg said.

"Him talking to me like that wasn't right!" Bookman shouted. "They can't talk to me like that!"

Berg tried to calculate the right response to get Bookman back on the job, but when Bookman got like this, well, there was nothing he could say to bring his partner around. "You gotta figure this comes with the territory," he finally decided to say.

"What territory?" Bookman said before he realized he knew the territory Berg meant. "Ok, so it's you too? *'E tu, Brute?'*"

"What are we, going back to ancient Greece now? First with *The Iliad* and now this?"

"It's Roman, you Philistine," Bookman said.

"I'm not jumping on any bandwagon, Bookman. But you've got to let it go. We have a crime to solve. A nice, juicy murder case."

"I can't let it go."

"Fine," Berg said. "Fine. Well, how 'bout this. You don't have to come back to work, but you can work the case with me in a private capacity. As a consultant."

Berg watched as Bookman rubbed the fingers of his right hand against its thumb. He was itching for a drink. This always worked to get Bookman back in the flow of the job. After a while, he would pretend that the insult had never occurred, that he had never been fired, never quit, was never suspended, never offended.

"I could use a drink," Berg said. "Have you got anything around here?"

"There might be something in the cabinet," Bookman said.

Berg went to the cupboard where Bookman kept his stash. He took down the bottle of Old Granddad and a couple of shot glasses.

"Here's to Ms. Pinkus," Berg said when he'd handed Bookman his dose. "May we avenge her death by finding her killer." They both turned the bottoms up on the glasses. Bookman handed his to Berg, who took them back to the kitchen and placed them in the sink.

"Have they found the bullet yet?" Bookman asked.

"Bookman, you sly dog," Berg said. "You've already been down to the crime scene."

"You may make a first-rate detective yet," Bookman said.

"No bullet," Berg said. "And no marks where it was dug out of the walls. This is old school, Bookman. It's going to take a better detective than me to solve this one."

Bookman clicked off the set and looked at his watch. It was 5:30 in the afternoon. "We've got a book club to go to."

Berg said, "Now we're getting somewhere."

"Hey, Bookman, check this out."

"I'm not listening."

> *"Everybody in the world is seeking happiness—and there is one sure way to find it. That is by controlling your thoughts. Happiness doesn't depend on outward conditions. It depends on inner conditions."*

Berg flipped the book over to look at its cover. "That's from How to Win Friends and Influence People, *Revised Edition."*

"Fascinating, I'm sure."

Chapter 2

Berg rang the doorbell and when after a minute or two nobody came, he and Bookman stepped inside.

"Hi," a large-breasted woman said. "I'm Delores. I'm *Men Are from Mars, Women are from Venus.*"

"But of course you are," Bookman said.

"You're new here. What's your book?"

Berg showed her his badge and so did Bookman.

"Are you the owner of this house, ma'am?" Berg asked.

"Oh, no," she said. "What's this all about? Was there a disturbance or something?"

"No, ma'am," Berg said. "We're looking for a Todd Gack."

"Sure," she said. "Just a minute." Delores twisted the end of her hair around her finger and gave Berg one more long look.

The entryway was short, too short for the house, so Berg and Bookman sauntered forth, toward the voices and the low jazz music, to get a better look at things. At the end of the hall was a big room with a high ceiling. The group, not small, was too small for the space. There wasn't enough furniture or pictures and the place had a new-paint feel to it. A man lived here alone.

The kitchen was at the far end and the covered dishes were lined up on the buffet. A few individuals where milling around them with plates in their hands. Some were lounging around the sectional in the middle.

A hallway on the left led back to what must have been living quarters and after a moment, Delores came out of it with a bearded man in tow. He was wearing a silk oriental crimson robe over the same colored pajamas. His hands were pushed down into the robe's pockets, helping to hold it closed.

"Did we wake you?" Bookman asked.

"Oh, he wasn't asleep," Delores said. "Todd meditates for over two hours every day."

"Even during the book club?" Berg asked.

"Especially during the book club," Delores said. "He says it's the best thing he can possibly contribute, don't you, Todd? Well, that and the use of the house."

"That'll do, Delores," Todd said. "How can I help you?"

Berg said, "We're detectives Bookman and Berg, Plimpton Police. You're Todd Gack?"

"That's right."

"We'd like to ask you a few questions, Mr. Gack."

"Concerning what?"

When Gack made no move toward a more private location, Berg held out a picture he'd taken from the house of the victim. "Do you know this woman?"

"Has something happened to her?" Gack asked without emotion.

"Oh my God, that's Sue Ellen," Delores said. With that announcement the other book-clubbers gathered round. Someone turned off the music.

"So you do know her," Berg pursued.

"Yes," Todd Gack said. "We all know her. She's part of the book club."

"She's *The Power of Positive Thinking*," Delores said.

"Not anymore," Bookman said. "Ms. Pinkus was found dead in her home this morning."

"Oh, no," cried Delores, suddenly unsteady on her feet. She swooned into Berg's arms. One of the men in the group rushed up to help him hold her upright. Bookman kept his eye on Gack. He was unmoved by the news.

"I never thought she was immortal," he said.

"You son of a bitch!" cried one of the women, moving to the center of the group. "If that's all your precious Tolle has to offer, I don't want any part of it!"

Without retort, Gack turned and walked back down the hall toward his bedroom.

"Oh, sure!" the belligerent woman said. "Go on

back and meditate, why don't you!" Whereupon she broke into tears.

One of the men tried to calm her down. "No one can know what his state of mind is right now, Noreen. People express themselves differently during times of extreme grief." By way of explanation, he added, "I'm *When Bad Things Happen to Good People.*" He had a pock-marked Arabic face with ominous, brooding eyes.

"What's she talking about?" Bookman asked.

"Todd is Eckhart Tolle," the consoling man said. "*The Power of Now* and *A New Earth.* He get's two books because it's his house. It's been a bit of a bone of contention around here. I think he just doesn't want anyone else to have Tolle."

"I'm not sure I understand," Berg said.

Another man, wearing a denim vest, chimed in: "Apparently, Tolle teaches that emotions like happiness and grief are two sides of the same coin. They both lead to suffering eventually, so they're both to be avoided."

"What do you mean, 'apparently'?" Bookman asked. "Haven't you read it?"

"Oh, no," said the man, with a supercilious smile, and a head full of curly black hair to match. "I'm happy with my own book, thank you very much."

Berg: "And you are?"

"*As a Man Thinketh,*" he said. "It's one of the oldest…and the best, as far as I'm concerned."

"So when it's your book's turn, everybody reads it, right?" Berg asked. "That's the way a book club works."

All but the sobbing woman stood sheepishly shaking their heads.

Denim Vest said, "No one can seem to get anybody else to read their books." He looked at his feet for a moment, and then added, "But it makes for some pretty lively exchanges."

"A woman is dead, people!" the sobbing woman said. "Hello!"

"Who is she?" Berg asked.

"She's *Don't Sweat the Small Stuff*," Denim Vest responded. Almost in unison, the group that was now pressed up around the detectives like a choir of carolers turned down the corners of their mouths and shook their heads in minute and rapid approbation.

"Drama queen," one of the as-yet-unidentified mouthed.

"Oh, come on!" the woman said in argument. "This isn't small stuff! We're talking about a murder here!" Whereupon the others gathered roundabout were forced to agree, nodding politely with subdued sadness, as seemed appropriate.

Bookman had seen it before probably a hundred times: the true killer feigning the deepest remorse. "No one said anything about murder," he said.

With that, the woman stood up, straightened her skirt, wiped her eyes. "I guess I just assumed," she said. "Who wants cake?"

As *Small Stuff* traipsed off toward the kitchen, Bookman asked, "Is she on medication?"

"We think so," Denim Vest confided.

Berg said: "We're going to need to interview each of you individually. Could someone ask Mr. Gack if he has a private room we could—"

"Feel free to avail yourself of my study."

Gack was back, crimson-robed and looking none the more verklempt than when he had broken away.

"I'm sure you'll want to begin with me," he said.

Berg looked at Bookman for a quick confirmation: this was the guy. "Actually, we'll need to talk to you last," Berg said.

"Oh," Gack said. "OK. That's fine. No trouble at all. I'll be in my bedroom, meditating."

* * *

The interviews took less time than either detective had anticipated. Personal data, contact information. What did they know about the victim? How would you characterize your relationship to the victim? When did you last see the victim? Where were you on Saturday evening? Can anyone corroborate your whereabouts at that time? All the usual stuff. What made this case different were the books.

There were twenty-one different titles represented in all. *The Four Agreements*, *The Road Less Traveled*, *Creative Visualization*, *The Psychology of Winning*, *The Seven Spiritual Laws of Success*, *Walden*, *The Greatest Salesman in the World*, *The Prophet*, *Be Here Now*. The list went on and on.

There were a few notable titles absent, one of which Bookman brought up when they finally got to Gack.

"What about the Bible?" Bookman said. "That's the best selling self-improvement book of all time."

"Uh uh," Gack said. "No way. I'm not bringing religion into this. That's not what we're about here."

"So maybe a religious book gets in under the radar," Bookman said. "You didn't like it and you eliminate it the only way you know how."

"What are you talking about?" Gack said.

"Sue Ellen Pinkus was *The Power of Positive Thinking*. I know what that's about. Norman Vincent Peale was a Protestant minister. I read it when I was a kid. My father gave it to me. He was Protestant, my mother was Catholic."

"Bookman," Berg said.

"But you went the way of your mother," Gack said defiantly.

"That's right," Bookman said. "That's how I was raised. What of it?"

"All right, that's enough," Berg said. "Let's take it easy."

"I had you pegged for the once-a-day-mass type the minute I laid eyes on you, Detective Bookman."

"That's right," Bookman said. "You got a problem with that?"

"No," Gack said. "No problem at all. Just so we're clear."

"We're clear all right," Bookman said.

"And to answer your question, the admission of books is a gray area," Gack said. "It doesn't matter by whom a book is written. What matters is its content. In the case of T-POP-T—"

"Hold on," Berg said. "What's—"

"Sorry," Gack said. "It's an acronym for *The Power of Positive Thinking*. Or just T-POP for short."

"Oh," Berg said, scribbling that down in his notepad.

"We made an exception for T-POP based on its longstanding status as a staple in the self-improvement category. We couldn't have kept it out if we'd wanted to."

"'We'?" Berg said.

"Me," Gack corrected. "My house, my book club…"

"How do you afford a nice house like this, Mr. Gack?" Berg asked. "If you don't mind my asking."

Gack was seated behind the desk in his study. *The Power of Now* was close at hand. He slid it across the table to Berg.

"The secrets of an abundant life in its various aspects are all contained in here," he said.

"Just answer the question," Bookman said. He was standing behind Berg and he leaned into the light shining from the desktop lamp to make his point.

Gack pulled back at the sudden onslaught and after a brief delay admitted, "Trust fund. I'm a trust fund baby."

"Which means you have a lot of time on your hands," Bookman observed.

"Where were you Saturday night, Mr. Gack?" Berg asked.

"I was here, meditating."

"Can anyone verify that?" Berg asked.

"Meditation is usually something you do alone," Gack said.

"Or during book club meetings," Bookman interjected. Gack ignored it.

Berg: "Was there anybody else that you excluded from the book club?"

"How could that possibly—"

"Answer the question, Gack," Bookman said.

"We're just trying to get a complete picture," Berg said.

"Yes," Gack said. "There have been several."

Berg tore a sheet from his wheelbook and handed it to Gack. "If you wouldn't mind writing down their names and phone numbers, we would appreciate it."

"All right," Gack said, letting out a put-upon sigh.

"What was your relationship to the victim, Mr. Gack?" Berg asked.

"She was a member of the group."

"That's it?"

"That's it."

"Was anybody else at odds with her?" Berg asked. "Over her book selection or anything else?"

"That's absurd," Gack said, chuckling. "This is a book club. Nothing more. Books don't normally generate that kind of reaction in people, do they?"

* * *

Bookman and Berg were on their way out the

door when Berg put his hand on Bookman's shoulder.

"Bookman, wait," he said. He looked around the room. The books were scattered everywhere, on coffee tables and end tables, shelves and counters. "I think we should take the books."

"What do you mean?" Bookman said. "As evidence?"

Berg hesitated. "Yeah," he said. "Something like that."

"Don't be ridiculous," Bookman said. "The books couldn't possibly—"

"Humor me, Bookman. I want to take them."

Bookman's investigatory rationality militated against getting bogged down in the content of the books. There was simply no logical basis for believing that the expenditure of the time required to digest their content could possibly render a lead in the case.

That wasn't what this was about. The ink had hardly dried on Berg's divorce. After ten years and two kids, he'd taken it pretty hard. That's what this was about.

Bookman's rationality also led him to a practice of his faith that saw anything outside of Catholic dogma as an equally unworthy expenditure of mental effort. All this bogus pop-culture pulp fiction would only serve to lead Berg further astray.

Even so, Bookman's hardness had its limits, especially where Berg was concerned. There was something of a code. If a fellow detective plays the "humor me" card, the idea must be hu-

mored—maximum one per case. Bookman looked at him like he was crazy, then held out his
hand, waving him on.

"Listen, folks," Berg said in an authoritative
voice, expecting resistance. "We're going to need
to take a copy of each book as evidence."

"No problem," someone said. And the books
were gladly handed over. More than one person
agreed that they bought them by the box and
handed them out to anyone who seemed the
least bit interested.

As they turned to go, Denim Vest stopped them
one more time. He said, "She was a nice woman.
Find her killer, detectives."

"We'll do everything possible," Berg said. "Rest
assured."

"*Listen to this,*" Berg said. "*It's from* The Seven Habits of Highly Effective People. *It says:*

> "*I am not suggesting that elements of the Personality Ethic—personal growth, communication skill training, and education in the field of influence strategies and positive thinking—are not beneficial, in fact sometimes essential for success. I believe they are. But these are secondary, not primary traits.*
>
> "*If I try to use human influence strategies and tactics of how to get other people to do what I want, to work better, to be more motivated, to like me and each other—while my character is fundamentally flawed, marked by duplicity and insincerity—then, in the long run, I cannot be successful. My duplicity will breed distrust, and everything I do—even using so-called good human relations techniques—will be perceived as manipulative. It simply makes no difference how good the rhetoric is or even how good the intentions are; if there is little or no trust, there is no foundation for permanent success. Only basic goodness gives life to technique.*

"*What do you think of that?*" Berg asked. The books layered his desk.

"*I think you're wasting my time.*"

"*Maybe,*" Berg said. "*But what else have we got?*"

Chapter 3

Detectives Kruger and Hernandez sidled up to Berg's desk on the way to their own. Kruger picked up one of the books.

"*Women Who Run With the Wolves*," he read. And another one, "*Your Erroneous Zones*? What is all this? You trying to improve yourself, Berg?"

"Something like that," Berg said.

"Oh, so you *can* read," Bookman said. "I was under a different impression."

Kruger smiled his smooth, goateed smile and looked at Bookman like he hadn't heard him. Both he and Hernandez looked uncomfortable in their trendy knock-off suits, Hernandez muscle bound and constricted, Kruger slim and stringy; they would have been more at home in baggy hip-hop attire. Hernandez's face had been gnarled by teen acne.

"The Chief is looking for you two," Hernandez said.

"The Chief?" Berg said, his nose still in the *Seven Habits*. "What's he want?" He put that one down and picked up another.

"He wants to talk about your mishandling of the Pinkus case," Kruger said.

"Get the hell out of here, Kruger," Bookman said. "We're managing just fine."

"Got any leads?"

"We've got lots of leads," Bookman said. "What do you think all this is?"

"If you need our help," Hernandez said, "just let us know."

"Is it Thanksgiving again already?" Bookman said. "The kids always want to sit at the big table. Here," he said, handing Hernandez a sheet of paper. "Get down to a place called the Human Fund. The victim and her boyfriend both worked there. See what you can find out."

"I was just being polite," Hernandez said as he read the names and the address.

* * *

"Welcome back, Bookman," Chief Farkus said.

"I'm here against my better judgment," Bookman fired back. "But since you apologized—"

"I didn't apologize," Farkus said.

"Berg?" Bookman said. Berg came into the meeting with an open book in each hand, his nose buried in one of them, and that's how he remained.

"I didn't apologize because there wasn't nothing to apologize for," Farkus said. "I didn't fire you, Bookman."

"Well, something sure as hell happened here," Bookman said.

"Yeah, something happened. We were sitting here having a nice little heart-to-heart chat and then all of a sudden somebody hit you between the eyes with a two by four."

Bookman looked at Chief Farkus but his mind was on that moment. "Yes, that's right," he said.

"Look, fellas, I haven't got time for this." Farkus said. "What have you got on the Pinkus case?"

"It seems the victim was linked up with a book club," Bookman said. "A brochure for which was the last thing the victim reached for before she expired. We're looking into her relationship with some of the other members."

31

"A book club, huh," Chief Farkus said. "What about the boyfriend?"

"He checks outs," Bookman said. "Lots of witnesses put him too far away at the time of the murder. I just sent Hernandez and Kruger down to the victim's workplace to interview her co-workers."

"Any other leads?"

"Nothing physical. One of the neighbors saw a car out front. A Chrysler product of some sort, sedan, dark color. And we still have several interviews to conduct."

"The book club people?"

"That's right," Bookman said. "Based on alibis, we've eliminated all but five: *The Seven Habits of Highly Effective People*, *The Secret*, *Think and Grow Rich*, *How to Win Friends and Influence People, Original Version* and *How to Win Friends and Influence People, Revised*. And also the leader of the group, a guy named Gack."

"Wait a minute," Farkus said. "What's with all the books?"

"Oh, uh," Bookman said. "It's easier to keep track of members by the books they advocate. It's shorthand."

"What about this Gack?" Farkus said.

"He has a couple of books by a New Age guru, Eckhart Tolle," Bookman said. "We're keeping a close eye on him."

"Not that," Farkus said. "I'm talking about the case."

"Yeah," Bookman said. "We like him."

"Anybody else?" Farkus said.

"Over the months the book club's been in operation," Bookman said, "Gack has excluded a few books on the basis of irrelevance to the purpose of the group. It's caused some bad blood. There's *Rich Dad, Poor Dad*, and *Zen and the Art of Motorcycle Maintenance*. We've got an interview lined up with the former, but the latter skipped town on Sunday."

"Day after the murder," Farkus said. "Where'd he go?"

"She," Bookman corrected. Farkus groaned. "She went hiking in the Himalayas. No word on when she's coming back."

"We're probably looking for a male perp," Farkus said. "You paying attention, Berg?"

"Yes sir," Berg said. "I'm just running down a hunch here. Excuse me."

"A hunch? This business don't work on hunches," Farkus said. "How many times have I heard you say that, Bookman?"

"The book club is about these self-help books, so called," Bookman said. "He has the idea that if he can figure out what the books are all about, it'll give us a better understanding of the case."

"Bookman, are you feeling all right?" Farkus asked. "How many times have I heard you say that a hunch is as likely to lead away from the perp as toward him?"

"It's his idea," Bookman said. "Not mine."

"I don't want to hear any more about hunches, Berg," Farkus said. "Bring me some D-N-A. Do you understand me? Hunches are for amateurs."

"That's not necessarily true, sir," Berg said. "It says here:

> "The formation of hypotheses is the most mysterious of all the categories of scientific method. Where they come from, no one knows. A person is sitting somewhere, minding his own business, and suddenly...flash!...he understands something he didn't understand before. Until it's tested the hypothesis isn't truth. For the tests aren't its source. Its source is somewhere else.

"That's a book called *Zen and the Art of Motorcycle Maintenance.* Maybe you've heard of it."

"I have heard of it," Farkus said. "Just a minute ago when Bookman mentioned it."

Holding up the book in his left hand, Berg said, "This one's by Eckhart Tolle, the one Gack's interested in. He says,

> "The surprising result of a nationwide inquiry among America's most imminent mathematicians, including Einstein, to find out their working methods, was that thinking plays only a subordinate part in the brief, decisive phase of the creative act.

"The Power of Now," Berg said, showing him the cover.

"That's what it says?"

"Yep."

"Is it footnoted?"

"Sure is."

"Get out!" Farkus said. "And bring me some

DNA!"

"Yes, sir," Berg said.

"And never rule out the boyfriend!"

"Hey Bookman, listen to this:

> *"Eddie Snow, who sponsors our courses in Oakland, California, tells how he became a good customer of a shop because the proprietor got him to say "yes, yes." ... Eddie described what happened:*
>
> *"A very pleasant gentleman answered the phone...He said he was sorry but they no longer rented bows because they couldn't afford to do so. He then asked me if I had rented before. I replied, 'Yes, several years ago.' He reminded me that I probably paid $25 to $30 for the rental. I said 'yes' again. He then asked if I was the kind of person who liked to save money. Naturally, I answered 'yes.' He went on to explain that they had bow sets with all the necessary equipment on sale for $34.95. I could buy a complete set for only $4.95 more than I could rent one. He explained that is why they had discontinued renting them. Did I think that was reasonable? My 'yes' response led to a purchase of the set."*

Bookman took off his glasses. "Are you just picking these at random to piss me off?" he said.

"No, no," Berg said. "I just find it interesting, that's all. I mean, I wish I had some of these techniques when I was still married.

Bookman put his glasses back on and went back to scanning Sue Ellen Pinkus's credit card records. "You gotta move on," he said.

Chapter 4

"What have you got?" Berg said.

A girl approached his desk from out of the open

bay office.

"The report you asked for," she said, laying it on his desk without looking up.

Bookman: "What's this?"

"I asked Ruthie to put together a report on the history of self-improvement books?"

"Who are you?" Bookman asked.

Ruthie's eyes widened, unsure how to respond. "Me?" she answered, holding her hand over her heart. "I'm Ruthie."

"She's an intern from the University."

"We have interns?"

"Only for about 20 years, Bookman."

"Why are you wasting her time with that?"

"It was my idea," Ruthie said. "I have to do a report on something to get credit for the class. The semester's almost over, so..."

"Shouldn't it be about police work?"

"This is police work," Berg said. He picked up the report. "We're policemen and we're at work. So what's it say?"

"Oh," Ruthie said. A pretty girl, thin with slumped shoulders, Ruthie was unaware there would be an oral presentation required. "Well. Self-improvement books have been around a long time. There were the *Analects of Confucius*, written around 450 BCE."

"Or just BC," Bookman said. "That stands for Before Christ, you know."

"In the western world, it's hard to say for sure but if you categorize all of Greek thought as philosophy, the first self-improvement book was called *The Enchiridion*, which means 'Manual' or

'Handbook,' by Arrian, who was a pupil of a Roman Stoic philosopher named Epictetus in the second century CE."

"Or AD," Bookman said.

"Epictetus was quoted by the Roman Emperor Marcus Aurelius in his *Meditations*, which could also be considered a self-improvement book. He was Roman Emperor from 161—" bowing a little toward Bookman, "AD—until his death in 180. He was also a Stoic philosopher."

"Interesting," Berg said.

"Yeah," Ruthie agreed. "During the Middle Ages, the most important self-improvement book was called *The Consolation of Philosophy,* written by a Roman government official named Boethius while awaiting execution at the hands of the Ostergoth king of the Kingdom of Italy, Theodoric the Great, in 525. This was, like, a successor state to the Western Roman Empire? And Boethius was a nobleman and held political office until he fell out of favor with the king."

"Wow," Berg said. "Western Roman Empire. What's that all about?"

"I'm a little fuzzy on the history," Ruthie admitted.

Bookman explained: "The Roman Empire got so big and ungovernable that the Emperor Diocletian split it into two parts, Eastern and Western, in 284—AD."

"I didn't know that," Ruthie said.

"No one does," Berg said. "Except Bookman. He's into that sort of thing. Please," he said, waving his hand at Bookman dismissively, "continue."

"This book, *The Consolation of Philosophy*, was really big in the Middle Ages. It was like a handbook that went along with the Bible. From what I understand, Boethius was a Christian philosopher."

"I doubt it," Bookman grumbled.

"What do you mean, you doubt it?" Berg said.

"Boethius died a pagan. Nothing in that book but paganism."

"Anyway," Berg said.

"Anyway," Ruthie repeated, wide-eyed and taken aback by Bookman's mood. "The Islamic world also has self-improvement books. The most famous was written in 1097 by a Persian Imam named al-Ghazali called *The Alchemy of Happiness*."

"Interesting," Berg said.

"Yeah," Ruthie agreed. "In American literature, self-improvement books began with Benjamin Franklin's autobiography. Then in the 19th century, there were the essays of Ralph Waldo Emerson and Henry David Thoreau, which could be considered self-improvement in nature. As far as the modern self-improvement book is concerned, *How to Win Friends and Influence People* by Dale Carnegie was the one that started it all off, followed quickly by *Think and Grow Rich* by Napoleon Hill. In the fifties, it was Norman Vincent Peale's *The Power of Positive Thinking*. The sixties and seventies saw a real explosion of these kinds of books. Too many to name. The best selling self-help book today is *The Seven*

Habits of Highly Effective People by Stephen Covey. Of those published this millennium it's *A New Earth* by Eckhart Tolle because of Oprah."

"Oprah, huh," Berg said.

"Yeah, she loves Eckhart Tolle."

"Ok," he said. "Great report."

"If you want to know more," Ruthie said, "there's actually a professor in the University English Department who specializes in this genre."

"Really," Berg said. "Is that where you got all this information?"

"This is all on the internet," she said. "I wouldn't go to Dr. Kramer, Babs Kramer, if my life depended on it."

"Why do you say that?" Berg asked.

"Because it's hard to believe she studies these kinds of books. She hasn't gotten anything out of them, that's for sure. She's mean-spirited, unhealthy, over-weight, petty. Really foul."

"Why am I not surprised?" Bookman said.

"Check this out:

> *"[T]here is nothing you can do to become free of the ego. When that shift happens, which is the shift from thinking to awareness, an intelligence far greater than the ego's cleverness begins to operate in your life.*
>
> *"Only the first awakening, the first glimpse of consciousness without thought, happens by grace, without any doing on your part. If you find this book incomprehensible or meaningless, it has not yet happened to you. If something within you responds to it, however, if you somehow recognize the truth in it, it means the process of awakening has begun. Once it has done so, it cannot be reversed, although it can be delayed by the ego.*

"That's from a book called A New Earth. *What do you think? Bookman? Bookman?"*

Chapter 5

"Pardon the mess, gentlemen." Steve Genderson met Bookman and Berg at the door to his office. He was dressed in suit and tie, as was appropriate to his position as a stock broker in the mid-size regional firm of Howbarth and Lowe. "I'm having my new office renovated," he said. "Let's go to the conference room."

Bookman loitered behind a moment as Genderson led Berg toward the room a couple of doors down the hallway. Drop cloths covered the desk and chairs, masking tape protected the moulding, the door was unhinged and leaning against the wall. Bookman took a closer look at the letters painted on the glass panel of the door in old-school fashion: Stephen J. Genderson, Managing Partner.

On the way in, Berg had pointed to Genderson's name on a sign in front of a parking spot with a black Jeep Commander parked in it.

"Is that your Jeep parked out there?" Bookman asked from the door of the conference room. Genderson and Berg were just sitting down.

"My spot, my Jeep," Genderson said.

"Any other cars?" Bookman pursued.

"No, that's more than enough car for me," Genderson said, smiling. When he saw that Bookman's line of questioning was complete for the moment, he filled the ensuing pause: "I was so sorry to hear about Sue Ellen."

"You knew her pretty well, then?" Berg surmised by his tone.

"I'm not sure I would say I knew her well. Sue Ellen could be enigmatic."

"Had you ever been to her house?" Berg asked.

"Oh, yes," Genderson said. "Several times. She was fond of the dinner party, as people of her set generally are. I'm a working class guy at heart. But I put on a suit after hours when I have to. Potential clients tend to frequent those circles."

"Did you handle any of Ms. Pinkus's money for her?" Bookman asked.

When Genderson hesitated, Berg said, "You're in the clear as far as confidentiality is concerned, Mr. Genderson, now that the client is deceased."

"We can always get a warrant, if that's what you want," added Bookman.

"Yes," Genderson said. "The firm handled an

account for her. It wasn't a large one, and I didn't handle it myself. But as a personal favor to Sue Ellen, I kept a close eye on her money."

"We'll need to see all the records pertaining to her account," Berg said.

"For that, I *will* require a warrant," Genderson said. "As a formality."

"Of course," Berg said. "You know Todd Gack, don't you?"

Genderson chuckled. "Yes, I know him."

Berg: "How did you get involved with his book club?"

"It comes with the territory," Genderson said. "Todd has a lot of money, and people with lots of money tend to have friends with lots of money. That's how I met Sue Ellen, in fact."

"You're book was *How to Win Friends and Influence People*," Berg said.

"That's right," Genderson confirmed. "Revised edition."

"Why is that such an important distinction?" Bookman asked.

"It isn't to me," Genderson said. "*How to Win Friends* is just a book. I read it when I was younger and when I heard about Todd's book club, I bought a copy and showed up with it."

"But..."

"But there was already a guy there, a hefty fellow named Frank Romanowski, who had already taken it. When Frank saw my book, he got upset and started to make fun of it. He said the revision was just to keep the copyright alive and that the new material had ruined the character

43

of the book, and so forth. He said I would have to find another book for the club. Which was fine with me. But when Todd got wind of it, he decided to allow both versions, I think just to piss Frank off." Genderson smiled and added, "Which it did."

"Are you married, Mr. Genderson?"

"Divorced twice," he said. "Devoted father of three. Devoted supporter of two adult ex-wives," Genderson added with a smile.

"Was there any kind of romantic involvement between you and Ms. Pinkus?" Berg asked.

"Oh, no," Genderson said.

"Why is that such a strange question?" Bookman asked. "She's a good looking woman. You're a good-looking man, in a gaudy Wall Street kind of way."

"Thanks for the underhanded compliment," Genderson said. "Maybe you should be asking Todd Gack about that."

"Why?" Berg asked.

"Talking about people like this isn't my thing," Genderson said. "Especially when they're...no longer with us."

"This is a murder investigation," Bookman said. "Spill it."

"She had a boyfriend."

"Scott Drake," Berg said. "Even he knew it wasn't going anywhere."

"Even so," Genderson said. "Gack didn't like it."

"Are you saying they had a history?" Bookman asked.

"Oh, yeah," Genderson said. "Going back

awhile. And...I'm sure it was nothing, but..."

"What?" Berg asked.

"I'm sure it was nothing, but I arrived early to the meeting just prior to Sue Ellen's death, and she and Gack were arguing."

"About what?" Bookman asked.

"I don't know."

Bookman and Berg looked at each other.

* * *

Interrogation room downtown. Bookman and Berg called dispatch to have a patrol pick up Gack and have him waiting when they arrived. The uniforms found him at home and let him change out of his meditation-wear and into jeans and a sweater before putting him, uncuffed, into the back of their cruiser.

"Why'd you lie to us, Mr. Gack?" Berg asked.

"I live in the now," Gack said. *The Power of Now*? That's what Tolle is all about. Or as Thoreau put it, 'I have been anxious to...stand on the meeting of two eternities, the past and future, which is precisely the present moment.' She's not my lover now. That's what I meant."

"She's nobody's lover now, big shot," Bookman said.

"You knew what we were asking," Berg said. "And why."

"This puts you right in the crosshairs where you belong, Gack," Bookman said.

"The two of you were arguing a few days before Ms. Pinkus's death," Berg said.

"I guess Genderson told you that," Gack said. "Money's always at the heart of these things,

45

isn't that what they say? Genderson's all about money—completely identified with it."

"Money or love," Bookman shot back.

"What was the argument about?" Berg asked.

"The direction of the book club. I wanted to keep it pure. Sue Ellen kept bringing in marginal books."

"What makes a book marginal?" Berg asked.

"Come on, Detective Berg," Bookman said. "Let's stick to the script."

"I'd like to know," Berg said.

"It's hard to explain," Gack said. "It was hard to explain to Sue Ellen. That's why we were arguing, I guess. It all starts with Tolle and radiates out from there."

"Start with Tolle, then," Berg said.

"For crying out loud," interjected Bookman. "Why are we going down this road?"

"Tolle's books are a fusion using modern language of the essential elements of all the major religions. Central to his philosophy is his concept of the ego. The ego, as Tolle defines it, is 'a false self, created by unconscious identification with the mind.' There is more to you than your mind. There is more to intelligence than thinking. And the voice in the head, the internal monologue, is the voice of the ego, a semi-autonomous entity that controls you until you dis-identify from it."

"That's ridiculous," Bookman said.

"OK," Gack said. "Try this. Take a moment to listen to the voice in your head, that internal monologue." When both Berg and Bookman seemed to levitate a little over their chairs, uncomfortable that Gack was turning the tables on them, he lifted his hand and said, "Just hear me out. Listen to what it says."

Bookman shook his head in disgust as Berg sat quietly for a moment.

"Did you hear it?"

"No," said Bookman.

Berg: "Yes."

"And what did it say?"

"This is absurd," Bookman said.

Berg answered: "It was saying all sorts of things, like I'm not sure why I'm going along with this, and maybe this Gack fellow is a nutjob—"

"Now we're getting somewhere," Bookman said.

"OK," Gack interrupted. "That's fine. Now tell me: who was it who was listening to that voice?"

"What do you mean?" Berg asked.

"That voice was talking to someone. Who was it talking to?"

Berg couldn't answer. He sat there looking puzzled.

"You see, that is the beginning of your own dis-identification from the mind. That voice is not your voice, it's the voice of the ego, which is a semi-autonomous entity that lives inside the spiritual space that you are. If you'll take the time to monitor what that voice says to you continually, you'll realize that it's a predominately negative influence in your life. That's because it's completely conditioned by the past. You are not that voice. You—Alec Berg—are the one who is *listening* to the voice, to the ego. You understand

47

what I mean?"

"Yes, I think I do," Berg said.

"It's a parlor trick," Bookman said.

"And the reason your partner here couldn't hear it is because he is as yet completely identified with that voice, with his mind, his ego. To him that voice is who he is."

"You're crazy, Gack," Bookman said, trying to dispel his own discomfort with a chuckle. He had heard the voice, himself. He had heard it, indeed, and the revelation scared the bejesus out of him.

"But that's not necessarily his fault," Gack continued. "It's an act of divine grace that gives us the initial awakening, which often comes in relation to suffering. I'm going to guess that you've recently undergone some sort of difficulty, Detective Berg."

"Another parlor trick," Bookman said. "Everybody has just gone through some sort of difficulty, Gack. Are we going to sit here and listen to this?"

"Yes," Berg answered. "I have. I just went through a divorce."

"That's how it was for me, too," Gack said. "The pain of a break-up started the whole process. It led me to Asheville, North Carolina, where I met a one-legged man who was sitting beside me on a barstool in a jazz club one night. When a one-legged man on a barstool talks, believe me, you listen. He told me about Tolle and the rest is history. That's why we're here. That's why all this happened."

"A woman is dead so you can tell Berg here all

about Tolle?" Bookman said. "Maybe that's your motive, Mr. Gack."

"That's not what I meant and you know it, Bookman!" Gack shouted.

"Not so difficult to break through that thin veneer of enlightenment of yours, Gack. My money says that's what happened with Pinkus. She questioned your mushy theories and you tried to take her head off."

"You're crazy, Bookman."

"And let me tell you one more thing," Bookman continued. "There's a whole different philosophy out there and it's been around a lot longer than your magnificent Dr. Tolle. It's called the Catholic Church and it makes a whole lot more sense that you or he ever will."

"He's not a doctor," Gack said.

"He isn't even a doctor, eh?"

"No, he isn't," Gack said. "You just don't get it, do you, Detective Bookman? You don't. You and your mainstream religion can't hear wisdom even when it's shouting in your ears. You won't give it the time of day unless it comes out of some dreary, dusty, dead seminary. I guess it's just going to take more suffering before you finally wake up."

"Is that a threat, Gack?"

"Take it easy, Bookman," Berg said, standing up to fill the closing gap between the two men.

"It's more like a prediction," Gack said sitting down, collecting himself.

"Look," Berg said. "Maybe we should continue this another time. It'll give us all a chance to calm down."

"Preferably without the Knights of Columbus next time," Gack said. "Maybe that way we'll be able to get somewhere."

"Why, I ought to—"

"You ought to what?" Gack said standing up fully for the first time in the interview. "It's always little fireplug guys like you—"

"I'm afraid that would be contrary to protocol, Mr. Gack," Berg said, once again physically intervening. "What if you say something incriminating and only one of us were around to hear it?"

"The sound of one hand clapping in the forest," Bookman said. "Right up your alley, Gack."

"So you still think I did it, too?" Gack said to Berg.

"Goes with the job," Berg said. "Sit still for a minute."

Berg followed Bookman out the door. "So what do you think?"

"I think he's a nut," Bookman said. "But if we held every suspect who lied about sleeping with the victim..."

"True," Berg said.

"He'll slip up eventually," Bookman said. "We'll get him."

"Right."

Bookman looked at his watch. "I have some personal business to attend to."

Berg knew Bookman went to confession every week, though he never spelled it out. "We've got the other *How to Win Friends* guy set up for this afternoon," he said.

"Right," Bookman said. "Pick me up in about an hour at the corner of Cathedral and Tenth."

"Right," Berg said. "Okay." He stood leaning against the two-way mirror.

"What?" Bookman asked.

"Just one more question," Berg said, turning the doorknob.

"So what are you supposed to do?" Berg asked Gack, who arrested his pacing at the sudden entrance. "About the voice?"

"Ah, for crying out loud," Bookman muttered. "This was the question?"

"What are you supposed to do?" Berg asked. "Are you supposed to counteract the negative thoughts by filling it up with lots of positive thoughts? Is that it?"

"No," Gack said, moving around the table to stand in front of Berg. "See, that's where James Allen went wrong."

"James Allen?"

"He wrote a famous self-help book back in 1902 called *As a Man Thinketh*. He identified the same problem of the voice in the head and he came close to breaking the whole thing wide open. That's what he thought the answer was too, positive thoughts. But that doesn't work. It keeps the ego alive and eventually its negative momentum takes back over."

"Right, right," Berg said pensively.

"You've got to shut down the voice completely, stop feeding the ego and it dies. Not until Tolle came along did anybody understand this. Well,

Tolle and the Buddha. A-and the Hindu tradition."

"I haven't got time for this," Bookman said.

Berg nodded and was about to go.

Putting a hand on Berg's arm to stop him, Gack said, "And by shutting down the voice, you stop adding to the pain-body too."

"The what?"

"The pain-body," Gack repeated. "That's the term Tolle uses for the accumulation of past emotional pain that lives inside just about everybody. You could call it a semi-autonomous entity too. It's responsible for a great deal of unconscious behavior. It's effect is similar to that of the ego, but the difference is one of proportion. If a person's negative response to a given situation is out of all proportion to the thing that triggered the behavior—even to the point where it seems completely unrelated," Gack slapped his hand with the back of his other hand, "that's your pain-body."

"Hold on just a minute, Gack," Bookman said, taking the suspect by the shoulder and sitting him down in a chair. "You've just described what's been called original sin for two thousand years. Is that all this Tolle is doing? Changing the names of things to make it sound like a whole new religion?"

"Tolle would be the first to admit that he's not talking about anything new. And he has no desire to start another religion. You want to remain a Catholic? Fine. You want to call it original sin? Go ahead. But tell me, Detective

Bookman, what does your priest tell you about getting rid of this original sin, so called, huh? What does he tell you?"

"I'm not going to get into a theological discussion about the Eucharist with you, Gack."

"No, of course you're not. You know why? Because you don't know. You have no idea how to get rid of original sin and neither does your priest!"

"Says you," Bookman said.

"I can tell you how to get rid of it in three words," Gack said. "Are you ready?"

"Oh, I gotta hear this," Bookman said.

"Make it conscious."

"Make it conscious, huh?" Bookman said.

"That's right."

"Well that just makes a whole hell of a lot of sense, doesn't it."

"It makes perfect sense if you have sense enough to open your eyes to it."

"I don't have time for anymore of this crap," Bookman said and he stormed out of the room.

"We'll get back to you," Berg said, following Bookman out.

"Detective Berg," Gack said, stopping him at the door.

"What is it?"

"It isn't me you should be looking at."

"Who is it then?"

"I didn't want to say anything at first..."

Berg's shoulders slumped. He'd had enough of Gack's deflection routine. "Come on, Mr. Gack. We have a lot to do here."

"Joe Temple," Gack said. "You might want to talk to Joe."

Berg motioned for Gack to sit down again across the table. He took out his notepad and flipped through it as he sat down himself. "*The Seven Habits of Highly Effective People.*"

"That's right," Gack confirmed.

"What about him?"

"He had a couple of friends who wanted to bring in all of Covey's books."

"Covey's the author of..."

"*The Seven Habits* and a few others," Gack informed. "Dr. Stephen Covey. They wanted to bring in *First Things First, Principle-Centered Leadership, The 8th Habit*, the whole nine yards, right?" Gack leaned across the table and took the volume down a notch. "These are all just rehash books. They rehash the same ideas as in the first one. He was trying to take over the group, turn it into one big Covey-fest. I wasn't trying to hear that."

"Did you just say 'I wasn't trying to hear that'?" Berg asked.

"I have to admit, I may have stepped over the line with Joe. But I did it to prove a valuable point. You can't just give people seven rules and tell them to follow them so they can be more effective. It doesn't work that way. The transformation has to come first, from within, don't you see? From above. It takes a divine touch to ignite the awakening."

"So you somehow pushed him over the edge?"

"I'd really rather not say anymore that that,

Detective Berg. When you meet him, you'll know exactly what I'm talking about."

"I'm running out of patience with you, Mr. Gack," Berg said. "Maybe we should get Bookman back in here—"

"All right," Gack said. "All right. This isn't going to sound very good, I know. But...Joe is black, ok? He's African-American. So were his friends. I may have allowed him to harbor the misconception that they were not welcome because of that fact."

"You told him you didn't want him and his friends in the group because they're black?"

"Not me," Gack said. "That's just it. I insinuated that Sue Ellen felt that way—not in so many words, but..."

"I would say you definitely crossed the line," Berg agreed, making a note of it.

"I can only imagine what Joe must have been capable of at that point." Gack seemed to demonstrate true remorse. "But my point was valid. Why didn't the seven habits help him? He certainly wasn't thinking win-win after that. Joe has an incredibly heavy pain-body. Lots of African-American people do. Tolle says it's part of a collective, inherited pain-body built up over many centuries of enslavement, torture and death. It lives on in the present generation."

"Makes sense, in a way," Berg admitted. "When did this conversation take place?"

Gack paused. "The day before the...you know."

* * *

"Here's something you may agree with in The Secret, *Bookman:*

> *"Many people in Western culture are striving for success. They want the great home, they want their businesses to work, they want all these outer things. But what we found in our research is that having these outer things does not necessarily guarantee what we really want, which is happiness. So we go for these outer things thinking they're going to bring us happiness, but it's backward. You need to go for the inner joy, the inner peace, the inner vision first, and then all of the outer things appear.*

"See? It's not just a get rich quick scheme."

"That book is blasphemous," Bookman said.

Chapter 6

"Oh, okay. I get it. This is because I'm the only black man in the group. I guess that makes sense to you."

"Are you the only black man in the group?" Bookman said. "We don't keep track of that sort of thing. Thanks for letting us know."

"Actually," Berg intervened, "we're interviewing everyone from the book club."

"Where were you Saturday night?" Bookman asked pointedly, hoping to illicit more vitriol.

"I was out, that's all you need to know," Temple said defiantly.

"Look, Mr. Temple," Berg soothed. "We don't care where you were as long as it wasn't at Sue Ellen Pinkus's house between the hours of 9 and

11. So if you can help us out with someone who can verify your whereabouts we would really appreciate it."

"What is this, the good cop/bad cop routine already? I know my rights."

"Just calm down, Mr. Temple," Berg said.

"You call me at my place of work and ask me to come here and talk to you and then you tell me to calm down?"

They were seated at the food court of Plimpton's largest shopping mall. Bookman and Berg had taken off their overcoats when they entered the massive, overheated space and sat down. Berg purchased a couple of soft drinks while they waited. A few minutes later, a portly black man in a well-tailored plum-colored suit walked purposefully toward them. When Bookman and Berg stood to offer their badges, Joe Temple told them to put those away and to sit down.

"This mall is a small town," Temple said. "There are eyes everywhere. And I happen to be the manager of the largest department in the largest store on the premises. I have a reputation."

"And the *Seven Habits* helped you get to where you are today," Berg parried.

Temple was taken aback. "That's right," he said.

"Maybe you could take a few minutes and tell us a little bit about the book," Berg said.

"Here we go again," Bookman mumbled.

Joe Temple was put at ease, though. He was no different from all the other book club members when it came to his book.

"The difference between *The 7 Habits* and all the other self-improvement books out there is its stress on the character ethic over the personality ethic. This is a significant paradigm shift, as Covey calls it. Techniques to win friends and influence people—the personality ethic—provide shallow, short-term results. When you stress character, those are changes that will last a lifetime."

"So it's kind of a *Seven-Habits*-versus-*How-to-Win-Friends-and-Influence-People* kind of a thing, then," Berg offered.

"Ex-actly," Joe Temple said. "Habit number one is 'Be Proactive.' What we mean by that is that you have to focus on your area of influence, as opposed to your area of concern, see. We all have all sorts of things out there that we're concerned about, right?"

"Right," Berg agreed.

"Most of those things we don't have any control over. So what's the point in paying any attention to those things whatsoever? The effective person focuses exclusively on those things over which he or she exercises some degree of control. See what I mean?"

"Makes sense," Berg said.

Joe was on a roll. He'd given this talk before. "Habit number 2 is, 'Begin with the end in mind.' If you don't know where you're trying to get to, the chances of you getting' there are slim to none. See what I'm sayin'?"

"Yes," Berg said.

"That's the way effective people do, see. They know where they want to get to and they develop a plan to get there."

"Makes sense too."

"Habit number 3 is, 'Put first things first.' That's the effective way to go about things. There may be a ringing telephone crying out for your attention. But is it the best thing you can be focused on at that given moment? Maybe yes, maybe no. So there's a little chart in the book that breaks it down for you. On one side you have Urgent/Not Urgent. And across the top you have Important/Not Important. See what I mean?"

"I think so."

"Some things are Urgent but Not Important. Like a friend calling to complain about his wife for the 57th time."

"Is this an example from personal experience?" Bookman goaded.

Just then Joe Temple's cell phone went off. He looked at it and turned off the ringer. "You got that right." He put it back inside his jacket pocket. "Other things are Important, but not necessarily Urgent. Like making it to your son's basketball game. Now that's important. But ain't nobody makin' you do it, see."

"Good point."

"Covey calls this a 'Quadrant 2' activity. Quadrant 1 are things that are urgent and important, like getting to the emergency room when you've broken your arm, or something like that. You basically have no choice in the matter. The effective person does his best to make enough time for important things that are not urgent."

"I never looked at it like that before," Berg said.

"Most people don't," Temple said. "The first three habits are designed to help people become more independently effective. They're personal in nature. The next three are designed to help people be more effective in an inter-dependent way, working and playing well with others, as they say."

Berg hoped Bookman was still listening.

"Habit number four is 'Think win-win.' Any time you're dealing with another person, whether it be in business or in a marriage or at church, we should always be thinking not only about how we can benefit from any given situation but how the other person can benefit too. This phrase has become so common in our language today. Everybody says 'win-win this' and 'win-win that.' 'Win-win situation,' 'win-win proposal.' All that started with Covey. But it's not just win-win, see. It's 'win-win or no deal.'"

"So if it's not good for both," Berg suggested, "then you don't do anything?"

"Exactly right," Joe Temple said, smiling for the first time. "I think you're catchin' on. You wait until you come up with some third way that nobody has thought of yet, that's what you do. That's called Synergy, which just happens to be Habit 6. I'll get to that in a minute."

Bookman bit his tongue. He was waiting for just the right time to lay in to Joe Temple, just the right habit to zing him with.

"Habit five tells us to 'Seek first to understand, then to be understood.' That breaks down barriers to communication. When the person you're talking to realizes that you've taken the time to understand his point of view first, they're much more amenable to listening to what you have to say. It kind of works in the background of their subconscious, see. But if you don't take the time to do that, the opposite will be happening in the back of they minds. They'll be saying to themselves, 'He didn't listen to me, why should I listen to him?' That's not in that person's best interests, but that's what people do. So you break that cycle by making sure that person feels like they've gotten their point across. You want to know the easiest way to go about doing that?"

"Sure," Berg said.

"Repeat back to them what they just said."

"So you're saying you should simply repeat back what the person just said," Berg repeated.

Joe Temple laughed a little, deep in his throat. "Now don't get slick with me, Rick," he said. "Yes, that's what you do. That gives the person a chance to clarify if you didn't get it right. Then you repeat that back to him until he agrees that that's what he just said. Then you tell him what you want to say, and he just might listen to you then. But don't do it sarcastically just to show him how stupid he sounds, you know what I'm saying? 'Cause that's not going to help the situation."

"That's good," Berg said. "Good advice."

"That brings us to habit 6, which as I said is 'Synergize.' It's based on all five that came before it, see. If you do all of those things, particularly habits four and five—"

"'Think win-win or no deal' and 'Seek first to understand, then to be understood,'" Berg repeated, referring to his notes.

"Right," Joe Temple said. "Then you're much more likely to come up with that third way, that third approach, that third solution that will satisfy both parties, that neither of you would have come up with on your own."

"Interesting system," Berg said.

"Habit 7 is 'Sharpen the saw.'"

"'Sharpen the saw,'" Berg repeated as he jotted it down.

"Covey says a person is composed of four aspects: physical, mental, social/emotional and spiritual. The effective person takes time to renew himself in all four of these areas regularly in order to keep his saw sharp. If you're all the time sawin' but never take time to sharpen that saw, you're not going to cut down the trees you have to cut down in life very effectively, now are you?"

"Guess not," Berg said.

"I guess not either," Joe Temple responded. "For your body, you've got to exercise, eat right, get enough sleep. For you mind, read a book from time to time. Socially and emotionally, spend time with friends and family, go see a movie. Spiritually, go to church or meditate, something of that nature."

Bookman said, "Were you thinking win-win

when you talked to Todd Gack about getting all your friends into the book club? Or maybe you were seeking to understand his point of view on the subject."

"That woman of his was a racist!" Joe Temple said, coming out of his seat toward Bookman. "She got what was coming to her!"

Bookman and Berg held their ground, looking at Joe Temple for a long moment, allowing him to realize what he had just said. Berg said, "Now do you want to tell us where you were Saturday night, Mr. Temple?"

"I am an elder in my church," he said with great indignation.

"Is that where you were Saturday night?" Berg pursued.

When Temple didn't answer, looking from one detective to the next and then back again, Bookman said, "I have a feeling you were engaged in something of which the congregation would not approve."

Joe Temple buttoned his double-breasted jacket. "You don't have anything on me." And he walked away.

When he was out of earshot, Berg said, "That could have been handled a little better."

"Of course it could have," Bookman said. "What do we care what he was up to, as long as it didn't have anything to do with Sue Ellen Pinkus?"

Bookman stood up, still looking in Joe Temple's direction. He was still in view down the massive corridor. Slapping his notepad against his hand,

Berg turned his gaze on Bookman once Temple turned a corner.

Bookman said, "Are you talking about him or me?"

Berg kept slapping his notepad against his hand. "Let's get out of here," he said.

"Bookman, listen to this:

> *"Public officials are often criticized for not being accessible to their constituents. They are busy people, and the fault sometimes lies in overprotective assistants who don't want to overburden their bosses with too many visitors. Carl Langford, who has been mayor of Orlando, Florida, the home of Disney World, for many years, frequently admonished his staff to allow people to see him, claimed he had an 'open-door' policy; yet the citizens of his community were blocked by secretaries and administrators when they called.*
>
> *Finally the mayor found the solution. He removed the door from his office! His aides got the message, and the mayor has had a truly open administration since the day his door was symbolically thrown away.*

"That's from How to Win Friends and Influence People.*"*

"Why are you wasting my time with this drivel?"

"The Chief's a public official. I think he needs more of an open-door policy too."

"I'm sure he'd be very open to your suggestion. Why don't you go tell him all about it? And while you're at it, read all these quotes to him and save me the trouble."

Chapter 7

Bookman crossed himself as he passed the altar, his leather soles rendering muffled clacks along the flags en route to the well-worn oak door of the confessional booth.

Inside was a kneeler, and a chair for those who could no longer make it to their knees. Bookman, though he could still kneel, sat in the chair and rested his head against the rear panel of the booth.

The first thing he noticed was the strong odor of gin. When it hit him, Bookman inclined his nostrils instinctively to get a closer smell. He breathed it in deeply: rotgut. He could just about make out the brand. Probably Boodles, if his calculations were correct.

What was that priest doing over there, drunk in the confessional? Bookman had half a mind to go over and yank him out of his comfortable box, give him a good scare like he used to do as a flatfoot on the beat to young punks on street corners. But you can't do that to a priest—dumb priest. Bookman knew deep down it wouldn't do any good anyhow.

"What have you got to tell me today, my son?" came the voice from behind the screen.

"You're drunk," Bookman said.

"Indeed, my son."

"No use confessing I put away a bottle of Old Granddad, myself, last night," Bookman mumbled, fingering the flask in his coat pocket.

"A priest is a priest is a priest, my son. You should be appreciative. A drunken priest is more likely to tell you the truth."

"Oh, yeah?" Bookman said. "About what?"

"About the faith, my son. That it doesn't stand up to intellectual scrutiny."

"Is that what this is all about?"

"At the end of the day, we're left with the Old Testament admonition: 'Honor God and keep his commandments.' Practice your religion and be done with it," the priest did his best to swallow a belch, "in other words."

Bookman sat in silence at this inadmissible confession, obtained under the influence of alcohol—he'd heard it before.

"We started up a whole new religion," continued the heretical homily, "that leaves us just where the old one did."

"Like hell, we did," Bookman said. "It's a system. Works like clockwork to get souls to heaven for anybody willing to do it. Couldn't be anymore reasonable. Watch what you're saying, pal. This is a church, for Christ's sake."

Father Justin Pitt had been Bookman's best—and these days, only—friend since well before the former added the clerical appellation to his name, though they refrained from telling each other of their respective affection except on those rare occasions—and only rarely even then—when Fate brought one face to face with the addiction of the other, as she was doing now.

Another minor goddess, Aidos, the personification of shame, kept them from ever drinking in tandem, a side benefit of which was the latitude for maintenance of a half-hearted denial, the symptoms presenting as simple, peaceful silence whenever they were together and in their normal functionality.

"You're late," Father Justin said.

"And I see how you managed to occupy the

time," Bookman said.

There had been a day when they had tried to "consider one another to provoke unto love and to good works." They had attended a few AA meetings in a nearby city, and that had helped for a while. But it made them both uncomfortable and had nearly ruined their friendship. And so they had drifted out of it, having been each other's only sponsor, returning to their semi-shared life of predominant semi-sobriety.

These days they shared the sacraments and little else. Father Justin, after confession or the early morning Mass where Bookman and a handful of blue-haired women gathered daily in a side chapel redolent with mold, candle wax and ash of incense, would retire to the sequestration of his brothers in the rectory, and Bookman to the isolation of his cell-like apartment to drink straight bourbon whiskey, read and watch TV. There was little difference in their lifestyles, except that Father Justin preferred gin and had to sip it most of the time on the sly. Bookman took his liquor openly at home and was only obliged to shadow his addiction beneath a cloak of secrecy while on the job.

"Something happened a few days ago," Bookman said, unsure how to get into this and whether he wanted to get into it at all. Best to put it out there now, he figured in the end, when Justin was more likely to forget all about it, if Bookman needed him to in the future, which was a very likely possibility. "I was standing in the Chief's office and he was talking to me about—well, you know what he was talking to me about. And out of nowhere it all just kind of went away. I don't know how else to say it. I felt...lighter. It only lasted a second. After that, I don't know. I quit or I was fired, I'm not sure which."

"So you're off the force?" the priest said, the news sobering him, completely missing the important part of the little narrative.

"What? No, no," Bookman corrected. "I'm back on. It was a misunderstanding, I guess."

"That's good," Father Justin said. And then there was silence for a while, broken by: "Do you realize that AA has a lower success rate than no treatment at all?"

"Yeah, yeah," Bookman said. He'd heard this before too.

"You stand a better chance of kicking it with no help at all," Father Justin said. "No help at all."

"I told you we shouldn't have gone. We'd be off it by now."

"Truer words were never spok'n," Father Justin said in his best Irish accent. "And the case? Have you anything good for me, John?"

"I'm working the Pinkus murder," Bookman said.

"Of course you are," Father Justin said, returning to his normal Plimptonite cadence, sharp and clipped, dulled only a little by the alcohol. "Big case. Need their best man on it."

"We don't have anything so far. Working on interviews now. She was mixed up in a book club, all self-improvement books. A jerk named

Todd Gack runs it."

"Todd Gack," Father Justin said, a burp emanating in conjunction with the surname.

"You know him?"

"Never heard of him."

"Rich kid. Nothing better to do. He looks good. He looks real good."

"Alibi?"

"No alibi but that's all we have. Berg has this cockamamie idea that the books are going to somehow lead us to the killer. Truth is, I think he's taking the divorce harder than I realized. He's looking at all this New Age crap for his own benefit. What he needs is Catholicism."

"A lot of good it's done you and me," Father Justin said. "Did I say that out loud?"

"But that sort of thing just isn't talked about on the force," Bookman said, ignoring the comment. "He knows my position. He would ask if he had any interest."

"You were meant to be a priest like me, John," Father Justin said. "That's your problem."

"Gracie ruined that for me," Bookman said.

"You could always get an annulment."

"On what basis would I get an annulment?" Bookman said. "All the sacraments were in place, I made sure of that. If I play that game, I become one of them."

"The Church is a woman, John," Father Justin whispered through the screen. "She hurts the ones who love her most."

The silence returned. Bookman thought about telling Father Justin more about his run-in with the Chief. But what more was there to say? Just start talking, something inside him urged. But he smelled the gin again and thought: this isn't working.

"What's not working?" Father Justin said.

"None of it," Bookman said, unaware that he had spoken his thoughts and unaware that he was still speaking them. "None of it's working. Look," he said. "You better close up shop until you've sobered up a little."

"You're the only one who comes," Father Justin said. "Otherwise, I'd be sleeping it off right now."

"Thanks for rolling out. Absolve me so I can get going."

"*Bookman listen to this. It's from* How to Win Friends and Influence People:

> "*Paul Harvey, in one of his radio broad-casts, 'The Rest of the Story,' told how showing sincere appreciation can change a person's life. He reported that years ago a teacher in Detroit asked Stevie Morris to help her find a mouse that was lost in the classroom. You see, she appreciated the fact that nature had give Stevie something no one else in the room had. Nature had given Stevie a remarkable pair of ears to compensate for his blind eyes. But this was really the first—*"

"*Do you mind?*" *Bookman said, more politely than usual. "While you've been improving your-self, I've actually been doing police work. I have Ms. Pinkus's bank records here and they're a little tedious, so if it's all the same to you..."*

"*I know how much you like Paul Harvey,*" *Berg said.*

"*Did it ever occur to you that maybe I've already heard them all?*" *Bookman said, looking over his reading glasses.*

Chapter 8

"Are you Kenneth Bania?" Berg said when the door opened.

"Kenny," the man said. He was dressed in a T-shirt and jeans. The over-warm air from the apartment hit Bookman and Berg in the face as they showed Bania their badges.

"We're detectives with the Plimpton Police De-partment," Berg said. "We'd like to ask you a few questions about Sue Ellen Pinkus. Mind if we come in?"

"No," Bania said, caught off guard. "No. Come on in."

He led them into a living room with a picture window down to the street. Off to the right was a kitchen with a table. In the corner sat a computer on a desk surrounded with books. Berg sat down on the couch, flipped open his wheelbook. Bookman stood facing the window.

"I heard about the, ah, you know," Bania said. "Her death. I didn't know what to do."

"What do you mean?" Berg said.

"Well, I knew her and I thought I should tell somebody but, you know. What was I supposed to do? Call up and say, 'Hey, I knew this person that was killed'?"

"How well did you know her, Kenny?" Berg asked.

"I knew her. Not well but I knew her."

"Where were you Saturday night?" Bookman asked.

Bania frowned. "My girlfriend said she wanted to spend some time with her friends. You know, a girls' night out."

"Pretty common," Berg said.

"Yeah, but on a Saturday night? It kinda pissed me off. Why can't they do that during the week?"

"Are you always this needy with women?" Bookman said.

"So what did you do?" Berg asked.

"I sat home," Bania said. "That's why I was pissed off. She didn't tell me until that day."

"Sounds like she's trying to tell you something, fella," Bookman said.

"Do you have any way to verify your where-abouts?" Berg asked.

Bania scratched his head through his tuft of curly red hair. His otherwise colorless complexion colored a bit. "No," Bania said. "I was working on a business plan for something I've got going."

While Berg was making a note of it, Bania started to say something but thought better of it.

"You wanted to say something, Kenny?"

"Well," he said. "I did get a pay-per-view movie Saturday night."

"Oh, I see," Bookman said. "The girlfriend isn't there to meet your prurient needs so you rent a little porn and play choke the chicken."

"No," said Bania, but he offered no film title to refute Bookman's deduction.

"I don't think that's going to help," Berg said. "But we'll check it out. You know Todd Gack, don't you, Kenny?"

"Yeah, I know him."

"Doesn't sound like you hold Mr. Gack in high esteem," Berg commented.

"That's 'cause he's a jerk," Bania said.

"The word on the street is that Gack wouldn't allow your book into the club," Bookman said.

"Yeah, that's right," confirmed Bania. "He said it didn't fit the criteria of the group. He lets in books like *The Secret*, but not mine. Do you real-ize there's a story in *The Secret* about a guy who says he can imagine great parking spaces into existence?"

"Really," Berg said, looking at his notes.

"He says before he goes anywhere he uses creative visualization to open up the ideal parking spot for himself. Yeah, right. What they don't tell you is...he's handicapped!"

"Really?" Berg said, chuckling.

"Well, I don't know that for a fact, but..."

"What's your book?" Berg asked.

"*Rich Dad, Poor Dad*," Bania said. "It really changed my life. Put it on the straight and narrow, so to speak."

"So what was Gack's problem with it?"

"He said it's a business book," Bania said. "Personal finance. Not broad-based enough. But if you ask me, money's at the heart of everything. 'Root of all evil'?"

"That's the love of money," Bookman corrected. "Not money, *per se*."

"Whatever," Bania said. "If people can just come to an understanding of the principles of money, they can solve a lot of their problems."

"Gack didn't buy that," Berg said.

"No, he just said it wasn't what the group was all about. But he lets in crap like *The Secret*. And *Think and Grow Rich*—that's about business! What's the difference?"

Bania was already getting worked up and he seemed to want to say more. Berg waited. One never knew what a person was going to say if you could get him talking. "This isn't just one book, you know. It's a whole series of books on all sorts of money related topics. The core books in the series are *Rich Dad, Poor Dad*; *Cashflow Quadrant;* and *Rich Dad's Guide to Investing*. I'd recommend those to anybody."

"Interesting," Berg said, and he really was interested. Seeing that, Bania's eyes lit up.

"Hold on a minute," he said. "I've got them in the other room." He darted off.

While he was gone, Bookman picked through the books surrounding the computer. *Business Plans for Dummies*, *The Complete Idiot's Guide to Business Plans*, *Business Plans Guide*, *The Anatomy of a Business Plan*, *An Exhaustive Illustrated Guide to Fletching*.

Bania came back with three purple paperbacks and handed *Rich Dad, Poor Dad* to Berg and *Cashflow Quadrant* to Bookman. He placed the third volume on the coffee table, where Bookman's ended up a moment later. Bania stood facing Berg with obvious delight.

"The most important principle is what it means to be rich," Bania said. "If you understand that, everything else falls into place."

Bania was smiling in anticipation of the inevitable question.

"So what does it mean?" Berg asked.

"I'm glad you asked that question," he said. "Are you ready for this?"

"I think we're ready, Kenny," Berg said.

"You're rich when the income from money-producing assets that you own—stocks, rental property—exceed your expenses. Once you reach that point, you're putting money in the bank each month without having to work."

Berg stopped flipping through the book and looked at Bania. "How's that work?"

"All right," Bania said. "Let's say you own five houses and they're all rented out for a thousand dollars a month. Let's say you spend only four thousand a month. That means you're putting a thousand dollars a month in the bank without having to lift a finger. *Er go*...you're rich. You reached critical mass, the tipping point."

"Oh, sure," Berg said, now drawn in. "But who has five pieces of rental property sitting around?"

"But you have to know what the goal is before you start, right?" Bania said.

"'Begin with the end in mind,'" Berg quoted. When Bookman looked at him funny, by way of explanation Berg said, "That's T*he Seven Habits*. Habit 3, remember?"

Bookman at length took his eyes off Berg and said, "Running five rental properties is a full-time job in itself."

"Not if you use a management company," Bania said.

"But that costs money," Bookman said.

"So you make five hundred instead of a thousand," Bania said. "The point is positive cashflow. In fact, that's the title of the second book in the series, *Cashflow Quadrant*." Bania pointed to the book Bookman had long since dropped on the coffee table as if it were hot.

"And jobs are for suckers," Bania said, that anticipatory smile on his face again.

"That from the book too?" Berg bit.

"Bingo."

"What's it mean?"

"It means you're never going to get to rich as an employee," Bania explained. "The tax code is set up to keep employees poor, while business owners use the tax code to keep from paying any taxes at all."

"Get outta here," Bookman said.

"It's true," Bania said. "Rich dad says taxes are the biggest expense people have. Most employees work half the year just to pay taxes. I'll give you an example. You guys probably get your cell phones and cars provided for you, but the average guy gets his paycheck every two weeks, pays taxes off the top and then has to pay his car payment and his cell phone bill with after-tax dollars, right? Not the business owner. The business owner pays the lease payment on his car and his cell phone bill as business expenses, and *then* pays his taxes."

"I didn't realize that," Berg said.

"Yeah, and the smart business owners soak up all the profits in legitimate business expenses— we're talking home office, business lunches, rent on office space, the whole nine yards—so he doesn't pay a single penny in taxes."

"Wow," Berg said.

"Yeah," Bania said. "It's a great deal. The whole system is all about limiting expenses and maximizing income-producing investments. Most people do it the other way around, which obviously doesn't make much sense. It keeps people poor. Rich Dad says the only reason to work as an employee would be to learn from the experience, to learn the business."

"All right, all right," Bookman said, coming to himself. "I've taken all of this I can take. How would you characterize your relationship to the deceased?"

"I knew her from the book club."

"That's it?" Bookman said.

"That's it," Bania confirmed.

"I think we're done here," Bookman said.

"Wait," Bania said. "Let me give you just one more example." Berg nodded. "You know how most people say that owning your own home is an investment?"

"Sure," Berg said.

"Well it isn't," Bania said. "It's consumption. That's what Robert Kiyosaki says. He's the guy who wrote the books. He says it's a liability because it takes money out of your pocket. An asset puts money in your pocket, see?"

"So?" Berg said.

"So don't buy too much house, and get it paid off as quickly as you can," Bania said. "That's the best strategy for getting to rich. Oh, and pay yourself first, he says."

"All right, all right," Bookman said. "That's enough for one day."

"Put money away for investment before you pay your bills, is what that means," Bania said.

"Would you mind if I hang on to these for a while?" Berg said.

"You can have 'em," Bania said. "I got a whole—"

"We know," Bookman said. "You have a box of

them in the truck of your car and you give them away to anybody who asks."

"Right," Bania said.

"Fanatics," Bookman grumbled. "Thanks for the advertisement. If we decide to try to get rich, we'll let you know."

"So what's your business idea about?" Berg said.

"What's that?" Bania said.

"Your business plan, what's it about?"

"I'm afraid that's a secret," Bania said.

"Come on," Berg said. "We're not going to tell anybody."

"No way," Bania said. "I'm not telling. I have a right to remain silent, don't I?"

"Take it easy," Berg said. "I'm curious, that's all."

"Are you a hunter, Mr. Bania?" Bookman said.

Bania looked at Bookman, mortified. He was standing by his computer. He looked down at the stack of books and turned the top one face down.

"Do you realize that Robert Kiyosaki made his first fortune as the inventor of the waterproof Velcro diver's wallet?"

"He invented that?" Berg asked.

"Yes, and because he didn't protect his idea, other people came along and made them more cheaply and put him out of business. He ended up homeless, living out of his car. I'm not going to let that happen to me. So don't ask me any more questions about my business plan. I'm not going to tell you anything."

Berg held up his hands. "Ok, ok, take it easy. It isn't important."

"Just one more question, Mr. Bania," Bookman said when they'd reached the door. "How do you know Steve Genderson?"

"Oh, uh," Bania said. "Isn't he in the book club?"

"So you only know him through the book club, then," Bookman said.

Bania shrugged. "I guess so, yeah. Through the book club. I think he's one of the *How to Win Friends* guys, if I'm not mistaken."

"That's right," Bookman said. He watched Bania thrust his hands into the pockets of his jeans and then rock back and forth on the balls of his feet.

"I, uh, better get back to my business plan," he said.

"Thanks for your time," Berg said.

When they were safely out of the building, Berg said, "What was that about Genderson?"

"Steve Genderson is Mr. Bania's broker," Bookman said.

"Really," Berg said. "How do you know that?"

"There was an envelope on the kitchen table with Howbarth and Lowe as the return address. Looked like an account statement. Howbarth and Lowe is a small brokerage house. The probability that Bania doesn't know Genderson even works there is low."

"Why would Bania lie about it?" Berg asked.

"I don't know," Bookman said. "Yet."

* * *

"Hey Bookman, check this out:

> "Roy G. Bradley of Sacramento, California, had the opposite problem. He listened as a good prospect for a sales position talked himself into a job with Bradley's firm, Roy reported:
>
> "Being a small brokerage firm, we had no fringe benefits, such as hospitalization, medical insurance and pensions. Every representative is an independent agent. We don't even provide leads for prospects, as we cannot advertise for them as our larger competitors do.
>
> "Richard Pryor had the type of experience we wanted for this position, and he was interviewed first by my assistant, who told him about all the negatives related to this job. He seemed slightly discouraged when he came into my office. I mentioned the one benefit of being associated with my firm, that of being an independent contractor and therefore virtually being self-employed—"

"So?" Bookman interrupted.

"So do you think that's the same Richard Pryor as the comedian?"

"All that so you could ask me that question?"

"Well..."

"Your time would be better spent going over these call records for the victim's cell phone." Bookman tossed the printout on to Berg's desk.

Chapter 9

There was always one in every investigation, a potential witness or suspect who wouldn't talk.

This time it was Lindsay Enright, a prim girl not long out of Plimpton U Law School. Bookman and Berg caught up to her en route to her brand new white Volvo. Designer overcoat, Italian leather briefcase, horn-rimmed glasses, she had the look. But when it came to the law, she was too green to try her hand at navigating the minefield of a criminal investigation.

"If there's one thing I learned from the one criminal law class I was forced to take in law school, it was this: never talk to the police."

"That's what they're teaching at the University these days?" Bookman said.

"Pretty smart," Berg mumbled. "I take it you don't do criminal."

"Contracts," Enright said. "Now if you'll excuse me," she said, "I have a client meeting to get to."

"No alibi?" Bookman said. "Nothing?"

"Sorry," she said, pressing her keychain to unlock the car.

"You knew the victim from the book club," Berg said as she closed the door. "You're book was *The Secret*, right?" he shouted through the window as the car began to move. When she was gone, he said, "I guess it really is a secret."

Bookman was already heading for the car.

"I guess I'll have to buy that one, myself," Berg said when he'd caught up.

"Don't let me see that on an expense report," Bookman said.

"I still say it's legit," Berg said.

"It isn't."

"What do you make of it?" Berg said, unlocking

the car door. "The cold shoulder routine."

"Could be something, could be nothing. We don't know yet."

* * *

The sun had come out and it was warm enough down by the waterfront for an interview. Frank Romanowski worked in one of the shiny high-risers nearby. Bookman and Berg met him by a pushcart. He'd just polished off a second hotdog for lunch.

"A handsome guy like me?" Romanowski was in his late-twenties. Though he was corpulent, he was dressed the hip urbanite, with the strap of a large pouch slashing across the black fabric of his squared off jacket. "That chick couldn't keep her hands off me."

"We're talking about a murder here," Berg said.

"I barely knew the woman," Romanowski said. "Let's just say she had a higher agenda."

"Meaning what?" Bookman said.

"Beautiful girl, lots of money. She's not much interested in a working stiff like me."

"What do you do for a living, Mr. Romanowski?" Berg asked.

"I'm a courier for a law firm."

"You're a courier?" Bookman said.

"Put me on a bike, I can go," Romanowski said.

Berg: "Which firm?"

"Connelly and Hobbs."

"Never heard of it," Bookman said.

"No criminal stuff, just mergers and acquisitions, stocks and bonds."

"You know your rival," Bookman said. "Steve

Genderson. Same line of work."

"He's in customer service," Romanowski said as a put-down. "I have nothing to do with him."

"Word has it you two don't get on," Bookman said.

"You're talking about the book club," Romanowski said with a grin. "That was vintage Gack. He likes to press people's buttons, that's all."

"It's pretty easy to press your buttons if you can get upset about a book," Bookman said.

"I don't see anybody else having to put up with somebody having their book. Why me? It's offensive."

"So why didn't you quit?" Berg said.

"Oh, no, that's just what they wanted me to do. I'm not falling for that."

"Is all this in the book?" Bookman said. "You're not striking me as one who influences a lot of people."

Romanowski took a deep breath. He was getting worked up. "I can turn it on when I want to. It isn't easy in a world full of fools."

"Fair enough," Berg said. "But you said yourself there was a big difference in the two books. Why not let Genderson in?"

Romanowski's face clouded. "What does this have to do with the murder anyway?"

"Nothing," Berg said. "We're just checking out everyone who knew the victim. Where were you Saturday night, Mr. Romanowski?"

"Again, a handsome guy like me? You have to ask? I was out with a hot babe."

"Home alone," Bookman said. "This seems to be

a familiar refrain for this book club."

"No, I'm serious, I was out with a hot babe. I'll give you her number, you can check it out."

They came to a couple of metal park benches backed up to adjacent tree boxes facing each other. They sat down there.

"Why don't you tell us a little about your book," Berg said.

"We don't have time for this," Bookman said.

But Romanowski reached into his pouch and pulled out a copy and handed it to Berg. "Here," he said. "You can read it for yourself."

"I already have one," Berg said.

"You have the revision," Romanowski said. "This is hard to come by. Check it out and decide for yourself what was going on with that piece of crap revised edition. It was all about the money."

"All right," Berg says, taking the book in hand.

* * *

When Romanowski had gone, Bookman said, "What are you going to do, read both books?"

"I was kind of hoping you might take one and I'll take the other," Berg said.

"I don't think so," Bookman said. "You're on your own with this goose chase."

Just then, Detectives Kruger and Hernandez rolled to a stop along Waterfront Road. Hernandez was behind the wheel of his personal vehicle, a black Chrysler. Rather than blow the horn, he turned up the bass on his music, knowing it would get a rise out of Bookman, which it did. Bookman and Berg walked the fifty feet of park to where the Chrysler sat partially blocking one of the two lanes of traffic heading northbound.

"What have you got to play that crap for?" Bookman barked. "You know you're blocking traffic."

"You gonna give me a ticket?" Hernandez asked with a mirthful smile. He turned down the music.

"We're done with the Human Fund," Kruger said. "Everybody checks out."

"Everybody?"

"It's a small office," Hernandez said. "Only five people in it. Four now. They were all pretty broken up. We ran down all the alibis, they check out."

"You drove all the way down here to tell us that?" Bookman said.

"Wanted to let you check out my new ride," Hernandez said, turning the music back up.

"Get the hell out of here," Bookman said.

"It's nice," Berg said. "What, are you taking payoffs again?"

"If you need anything else, let us know," Kruger said from the passenger seat as Hernandez eased the Chrysler back into the flow of traffic.

Berg scribbled a couple of lines on a page in his wheelbook. "Here," he said, ripping it out and hurrying to catch up to Kruger's outreached palm. "Find out what you can about Lindsay Enright. She's a lawyer at Sagman, Bennett."

Kruger waived the paper as the Chrysler picked up speed.

* * *

"Listen to this, Bookman:

"In his book Getting Through to People, *Dr. Gerald S. Nirenberg commented, 'Co-operativeness in conversation is achieved when you show that you consider the other person's ideas and feelings as important as your own. Starting your conversation by giving the other person the purpose or direction of your conversation, governing what you say by what you would want to hear if you were the listener, and accepting his or her viewpoint will encourage the listener to have an open mind to your ideas.'*

"That's from the revised How to Win Friends.*"*

"Really," Bookman said without interest.

"Gotta be," Berg said checking the original. *"Get-ting* Through to People *was published in 1963.* How to Win Friends *was originally published in 1937."*

"You're powers of deduction are really coming along, Detective Berg. He's talking about the Gold-en Rule. Nothing new there."

"I, uh, thought you weren't listening."

Chapter 10

Bookman and Berg drove from the waterfront directly out to the headquarters of Play Now, Inc.

"No wonder we never heard of this place," Bookman commented upon seeing the building. It was in an office park, small and nondescript, the front door of the Play Now office opening on to a walkway beneath an overhang, lined by short boxy bushes.

Berg opened the door, behind which sat a

plump, dark-haired woman in jeans and a sweater. In one motion, she looked up from the computer screen and used the mouse to click out of the game that had been occupying her interest.

"I see why this place is called Play Now," Bookman said.

"Hi," she said.

Berg said, "We're here to see Jacob Jarmel."

"Oh," the woman said. "Jake's not here."

"We had an appointment," Berg said, showing the woman his badge.

The woman stiffened. "Actually, he's been in an accident."

"Anything serious?" Berg said.

"I don't know," the woman said. "His wife called this morning to let me know, but she didn't have any of the details."

"Where is he now?" Berg asked.

"University Hospital."

As they were leaving, Bookman said, "By the way, what goes on here?"

"Mr. Jarmel is an inventor," the woman said. "He invents things. Gadgets, I guess you'd call them."

"Gadgets," Bookman said. "Thanks."

When they were outside again, Bookman said, "I think our case just got a little more interesting."

Berg stopped. "That's intuition," he said.

"What are you talking about?" Bookman said.

"You and the chief said I was crazy, but you both do it," Berg said. "Everybody does it."

"Does what? Berg, you're talking nonsense."

Berg started walking again, one eye closed, shaking his finger at Bookman. Something had come to him.

* * *

In his private hospital room, Jake Jarmel was in a full body cast, but he was conscious. A drug-induced smile spread across his face when Bookman and Berg entered the room. They showed their badges to a woman sitting in a chair in the near corner by the bed.

"Honey," she said, standing to hover over the patient. "These men are policemen. They're here to talk to you about the accident."

"Actually," Berg said. "We had an appointment with Mr. Jarmel to talk about something else."

"Oh, yes," the woman said. "The Pinkus murder. Under the circumstances, I think it would be better if—"

"That's all right, honey," Jake Jarmel spoke up. "It's fine. I'm fine. I'm happy to talk with them."

"What happened?" Bookman asked.

"He was hit by a bus," the woman said.

"Jeez," Berg said.

"No," Jake Jarmel said. "It's a miracle."

"That you're still alive, you mean?" Berg asked.

"Not that," the man said, under the influence of the pain-killers, suddenly turning sullen.

"You're his wife?" Berg asked.

"Yes," she said. "Elaine."

"What's he talking about?" Bookman asked.

She looked a little sheepish. "It's that book."

"What book?" Bookman asked.

"*Think And Grow Rich*?" Berg offered.

"Yes," the woman said. "How did you know that?"

"That's what we're here to talk about, actually," Berg said. "Your husband was in a book club with the victim, Ms. Pinkus."

"Oh, yes," Elaine Jarmel said. "That Gack fellow's group."

"Gack's cool," Jake Jarmel interjected, dreamily. "Gack's very cool."

"Try to relax, Jake," Elaine said.

"So what's the miracle?" Bookman pressed.

Elaine Jarmel glanced sideways at her husband. "It's such an old book," she said. "I have no idea why he's so attached to it."

"You read it?" Berg asked.

"I had to," she whispered. "He wouldn't leave me alone until I did. It has a lot of good ideas in it. But it also has some weird ones, like—what was the word? Sex transmutation, that was it."

"But the book was written in the thirties, wasn't it?"

"That was what was so weird about it," Elaine said. "I guess it was ahead of its time."

Jake Jarmel stirred to life again. "Andrew Carnegie was one of the richest men who ever lived," he slurred. "The book is about his secret to success. He might as well have written that book himself."

"Don't get excited, Jake," his wife said. "It's a great book, ok?"

"You're darn right, it is."

Elaine tilted her head in the direction of the

door. "Let's step out into the hall. I'll be right back, honey."

Once outside, Bookman asked, "So what's this miracle he's talking about?"

"The book is a whole system," she said. "First, it gives you a self-confidence statement to memorize, which is supposed to ingrain in you that you're capable of achieving whatever it is you set your sites on."

"Money," Bookman said, a surly expression on his face.

"Could be money, but it doesn't have to be."

"Go on," Berg said.

"Taking money as an example," she said, nodding to Bookman, "it tells you to pick an amount you want to receive. It gives you affirmations and tells you to say them every day. Something like, 'I can see the money in my hands, I can see it on my bank statement.' Stuff like that."

"So it was *The Secret* before *The Secret* was *The Secret*," Berg said. Bookman looked at him, incredulous. "I was reading that one this morning."

"Pie in the sky kind of stuff," Bookman said, putting his own spin on it.

"Creative visualization," Berg corrected.

"Not exactly," Elaine Jarmel said. "That's part of it. It says you've got to have a strong desire along with faith and creative visualization, as you call it. But it also has its practical side. There's a whole chapter on developing specialized knowledge, for example, and another one on how to write a resume. One on surrounding yourself with smart people, a mastermind group. What it takes to be a good leader, like attention to detail, loyalty. A lot of good stuff in that book."

"Sounds like you're a convert," Berg said.

Elaine lowered her head. "For me it's just a book," she said. "But it's an obsession with Jake."

"The miracle?" Bookman reminded.

"Jake decided his goal would be five million dollars. He wrote out the auto-suggestion statement—"

"Auto-suggestion statement?" Berg repeated.

"That's what the book calls the daily affirmation. It's supposed to change your perception of what's possible, of what's reality, through suggestion. You say it, you hear yourself saying it. It becomes reality."

"Go on."

"He wrote it out and he made me memorize it with him and say it with him all the time. At least three times a day."

"And."

"And, you know, it kind of gets to you. I really started to believe it was possible after a while. Jake started working on his MBA at night. That took a year and a half. When that was done, we were in debt but Jake wanted to quit his job and start up his own company."

"Play Now," Berg said.

"Play Now, that's right. At first I was hesitant, of course. We have two kids and I was afraid things might not work out. Jake made me re-

read the chapter on fear and he was so sure of what he wanted to do—it's called having a definite purpose in the book—that I eventually said yes."

"Honey!" Jake was calling from inside the room.

"Coming," Elaine said. "And that was three and a half years ago."

When she had pushed inside the door, Bookman said, "I still don't know what the miracle is."

"What's going on out there, honey?" Jake said. "What are you telling them?"

"I'm telling them all about your favorite book," she said.

"Oh, right," he said. "Elaine is my source of sex transmutation."

"Jake!"

"What does that mean?" Bookman said.

"I think a better way to say it is, 'Behind every great man...'" Elaine said, lowering her head.

"'Is a great woman,'" Berg finished.

Bookman: "And behind every great woman is a great—"

"Bookman," Berg said.

But Jake Jarmel chimed in, "You got that right, mister," at which point he nodded off to sleep.

"So what's the miracle?" Bookman persisted.

Looking again at her husband, this time worry vexing the grace of her features, she said, "Our lawyer has already been to visit. You just missed him, in fact."

"And," Bookman pressed.

"And he said this accident would be worth

more than a million dollars, easily."

Both Berg and Bookman involuntarily nodded and shrugged.

"Probably true," Berg said.

"Easily," Bookman agreed. "But how is that a miracle?"

"So far, Jake's made $4 million at Play Now," Elaine said.

"Making gadgets," Bookman said. "That *is* a miracle."

"Another million puts him past his *Think and Grow Rich* goal."

"Wow," Berg said. "That *is* interesting."

"That's not the interesting part," she said. "The book also tells you to set a definite date for your goal."

"What was the date?" Berg asked.

She looked at Jake and then at the detectives. "Tomorrow."

Just then a couple of nurses came in and asked the detectives for some privacy.

"One more question," Berg said. "We have to ask. Where was Jake on Saturday night?"

"We were together at a fundraiser for a friend's nonprofit. Lots of people. We were home at three in the morning. Our babysitter can tell you."

"We have to ask," Berg said.

* * *

Outside the room, Berg said, "Do you need any more proof?"

"Of what?" Bookman asked.

"That this stuff works."

"Don't you see what's going on here?" Bookman

said, stopping Berg. "This guy did this on purpose so he could reach his goal."

"Come on, Bookman," Berg said. "You think he stepped in front of a bus so he could reach his goal? That's crazy."

"I think that's exactly what he did and I'm going to see to it that he doesn't get away with it."

Bookman started walking again, putting his cell phone to his ear.

"Come on, Bookman. Look at the guy, he's in a body cast. This has nothing more to do with us. Why don't you leave it alone?"

"It has everything to do with us," Bookman reacted.

"How? How does this have anything to do with us?"

Bookman stopped again, striking a pugnacious pose, sticking his bulbous red snout up as close to Berg's more attractive features as his stature would allow. "We're city employees."

"Yeah, so."

"That was a city bus. We have a responsibility to our employer to see that it isn't taken for a ride."

"You know what I think?" Berg said. "I think you're threatened by the idea that these books may have something that you don't understand."

"Don't be ridiculous," Bookman said. "I'm just doing my duty as a public employee, that's all."

He began walking again. When dispatch came on the line, a large black orderly said, "You can't use cell phones in here."

Bookman started to argue until he laid his angry, bloodshot eyes on the large man himself, at which point he flipped shut his phone and jammed it into the pocket of his overcoat. Just then he watched as a man in a suit knocked on Jarmel's door.

"We'll take care of this right now," Bookman said and he hurried up to the man.

"Are you Jake Jarmel's attorney?" he said, flashing his badge.

"No," the man said. He took a card from his jacket pocket and handed it over: Adam Lippman, it read. "I'm with Pendant Publishing," Lippman said. "When Mr. Jarmel's publicist called, I came right away."

"He has a publicist?" Bookman said.

"His company does," Lippman said. "*Think and Grow Rich* is one of our backlist titles. We found the angle she pitched irresistible."

"Oh, really," Bookman said. "How do you like this angle? He's not going to make it to his goal. I'm going to see to that because he did this on purpose. No court in the world is going to give him any money."

"We'll see about that," Lippman said, looking down his nose at Bookman. "But to tell you the truth, that's an even better twist ending. Mean little police detective keeps visionary from goal. Only to have the book itself carry him across the finish line. It's like a fairy tale, isn't it? This book will make well over a million, I'll stake my reputation on it."

"Oh really?" Bookman said.

"Yes."

"The deadline's tomorrow. How are you going to get around that?"

Lippman reached into his suit pocket. "We're prepared to pay Mr. Jarmel a substantial advance. I happen to have the check right here."

Bookman took it, looked at it, handed it back. "This isn't for a million dollars."

"Of course it isn't," Lippman said. "I've been on the phone with Mr. Jarmel's accountant for the last three hours, establishing his net worth down to the penny. It seems he wasn't as far off as he thought."

Bookman ground his teeth.

"Now if you'll excuse me," Lippman said. "I need to get a contract signed."

"Go on," Bookman said. "A man's been severely injured, you know. You'd think his friends might be a little upset about that!"

When Lippman disappeared through the door to Jarmel's room, Bookman said through gritted teeth, "Get me the books."

"What was that?" Berg said with a smile. "I couldn't quite hear you."

"Get me the books!"

"Listen to this:

> *"You can dramatize your ideas in business or in any other aspect of your life. It's easy. Jim Yeamans, who sells for the NCR company (National Cash Register) in Richmond, Virginia, told how he made a sale by dramatic demonstration.*
>
> *"Last week I called on a neighborhood grocer and saw that the cash registers he was using at his checkout counters were very old-fashioned. I approached the owner and told him, 'You are literally throwing away pennies every time a customer goes through your line.' With that I threw a handful of pennies on the floor. He quickly became more attentive. The mere words should have been of interest to him, but the sound of pennies hitting the floor really stopped him. I was able to get an order from him to replace all of his old machines.*

"We've got to find a way to dramatize the importance of these books to the Chief," Berg said. "He still doesn't get it. Maybe we should stack them up all over his desk and—"

"What's it from?" Bookman asked.

"How to Win Friends."

"Revision or original?"

Berg flipped the book over. "Revision."

Chapter 11

Bookman sat down in his easy chair, the books stacked in front of him like cold cuts, a bottle of Old Granddad on the table beside him beneath the lamp. He poured a tumbler full and settled back. It was going to be a late night.

How could any of this pop culture psycho-babble possibly offer people any answers? Far from it, he had long since decided. This flotsam of a civilization that had lost its way was part and parcel of its demise.

And yet, he had to admit, Berg was right. Something told him they held the key to this case. Where that something came from, he had no idea—something Berg was right about too. It was more than just Jake Jarmel's story that had started him thinking. It wasn't logical. It was extra-logical.

Hold his nose and weigh in, that's all he could do. This was no different from all the times he'd gone dumpster diving for murder weapons and other physical evidence. It was part of being a cop.

The clear choice to start with was Eckhart Tolle. Gack was the favorite in the suspect race. Bookman needed to beat him at his own game. He started with *The Power of Now*, it came first. Preface, introduction, yada yada yada. Let's get on with it, shall we.

"Enlightenment–What is that?" read the first subtitle.

I'll tell you what that is, Bookman said to himself. It was an age when godless men decided to usurp the authority of the Church. That's what enlightenment was and is. Sure, there were some abuses going on in the Church in those day. Reformation, counter-reformation. But enlightenment has brought with it nothing good, I can tell you that much right now.

He'd barely gotten off the first subtitle and it was time for a drink. Half the tumbler of bourbon was gone before he'd finished his internal diatribe. He put the glass down without having realized that he'd picked it up and turned the page as he scanned.

"...the radiant joy of Being, and the deep, unshakeable peace that comes with it..."

He capitalizes "Being," how quaint. That can only mean one thing: that this Tolle character dares to equate "being" with God. What else could that mean? God is God. And the Catholic Church has long since defined Him in the catechism. End of discussion. Move on.

Another drink he didn't know he was taking. A pour he didn't know he was pouring.

"I love the Buddha's simple definition of enlightenment as 'the end of suffering.'"

Here we go with the Eastern stuff. I knew it! I knew that's what this was all about. Transcendental meditation, om and all that crap. Enlightenment is the end of suffering, huh? You can't end suffering. That's what life is all about. Ending suffering is what heaven was made for. These people just don't get it, do they. They don't!

"What is the greatest obstacle to experiencing this reality? Identification with your mind, which causes thought to become compulsive."

What kind of horses#@t is this?...This is the most ridiculous...If we are not our minds, then what are we?...

Bookman began to monitor what he was saying

inside his head, just as if they were words on a page.

What was it Gack had said? "Listen to the voice inside your head. What is it saying?" Gack is cracked, but...

Now Bookman couldn't take his inner eyes off his inner voice, his own stream of consciousness.

Another drink he didn't know he was taking. Another pour he didn't know he was pouring.

After some time, he'd worked his way from *The Power of Now* to the second in the Tolle series, *A New Earth*, subtitled *Awakening to Your Life's Purpose*.

Here we go again, thought Bookman. Same old stuff, different book. A little better organized, less dense, more to the point. By the time he'd worked his way to the end, Bookman felt like he understood the philosophy, even if he didn't agree with it, and that was the point of this pointless exercise, after all, getting inside Gack's head—*before he gets inside mine*, Bookman was drunk enough to tack on.

On the one hand, you have what Tolle calls the ego:

> In normal everyday usage, "I" embodies the primordial error, a misperception of who you are, an illusory sense of identity. This is the ego. This illusory sense of self is what Albert Einstein, who had deep insights not only into the reality of space and time but also into human nature, referred to as "an optical illusion of consciousness." That illusory self then becomes the basis for all future in-

terpretations, or rather misinterpretations of reality, all thought processes, interactions, and relationships. Your reality becomes a reflection of the original illusion.

The ego, according to Tolle, runs most people's lives, but it isn't real, it's an illusion. Knowing this, it does all it can to stave off its own death (i.e. awakening from the illusion that it is) by forming various identities that are meant to make it seem more real. It latches on to fancy cars, big houses and other material wealth to create the illusion of stability. But nothing in this "world of forms" is ever stable, says Tolle, so the effort always ends in failure—unhappiness, suffering—because all that is real is unmanifested, outside this world of forms. All that is real is inside each person.

These identifications can even be negative in nature. Some people identify with ailments and illnesses. The constant complaints define who they are, give them something to hold on to.

This is where the voice in the head comes into play. That voice is the voice, not of the person, but of the person's ego, as opposed to the actual person, who is the one who is *listening* to that incessant stream of verbal diarrhea.

Bookman needed a long drink after that insight. He took it. He poured another.

Then there is the pain-body, a "semi-autonomous entity" that lives inside of each human being. It's the accumulation of past emotional pain and trauma that was not fully dealt with consciously when it came up the first time. From time to time, this entity comes out of dormancy to take over a person's thought patterns, turning them sharply negative.

The emotional pain that makes up the pain-body can come from a person's own life, it can also be collective, or even hereditary.

> The pain-body...is not just individual in nature. It also partakes of the pain suffered by countless humans throughout the history of humanity, which is a history of continuous tribal warfare, of enslavement, pillage, rape, torture, and other forms of violence. This pain still lives in the collective psyche of humanity and is being added to on a daily basis.

Now what if ego creates an identity for itself out of the pain-body? That's when there's real trouble.

Wait a minute, thought Bookman. He had a suspicion that was only strengthened by the following passage:

> Whenever you get taken over by the pain-body, whenever you don't recognize it for what it is, it becomes part of your ego. Whatever you identify with turns into ego. The pain-body is one of the most powerful things the ego can identify with, just as the pain-body needs the ego to renew itself through it. That unholy alliance, however, eventually breaks down in those cases where the pain-body is so heavy that the egoic mind structures, instead of being strengthened by it, are becoming eroded by the continuous onslaught of the pain-body's energy charge, in the same way that an electronic device can be

empowered by an electric current but also destroyed by it if the voltage is too high.

Wait a minute, wait a minute! Bookman told himself. Do you see what's just happened here? This so-called unholy alliance he's talking about is just modern-day psycho-babble for the Catholic doctrine of Original Sin! This is all just repackaged Catholicism! This was exactly what he had told Gack before and he only confirmed now that he had been spot on in his assessment.

Bookman conveniently glossed over the following passage, however:

> All religions are equally false and equally true, depending on how you use them. You can use them in the service of the ego, or you can use them in the service of the Truth. If you believe only your religion is the Truth, you are using it in the service of the ego. Used in such a way, religion becomes ideology and creates an illusory sense of superiority as well as division and conflict between people. In service of the Truth, religious teachings represent signposts or maps left behind by awakened humans to assist you in spiritual awakening, that is to say, in becoming free of identification with form.

All right, all right, all right, thought Bookman. So what's Tolle's answer to this problem? Step one is to stop adding any more old emotion to the pain-body by making all thoughts and emotions conscious as they happen. This is the end of the ego, technically speaking (though it will still influence behavior for a finite period of time after awakening begins) since the term ego denotes unconsciousness. Once observed by the awakened consciousness, the ego simply becomes a negative mental pattern, rooted in the past, weakened almost beyond recognition, and someday soon entirely dissolved.

Step two: dissolve the pain-body through consciousness of it whenever it comes out to play.

* * *

A little later Bookman moved on to *The Secret*. It was the next logical choice. Ms. Lindsay Enright, Esquire, certainly seemed to have something to hide. Hernandez and Kruger had come up with nothing. After the Romanowski interview, Berg had stopped off at a Barnes and Noble and come out with *The Secret* in two forms.

"Comes as a book and a DVD," he said. "And it's a little pricy. No wonder she doesn't keep them in a box in the trunk of her car like all the rest of them do."

Bookman had taken the DVD.

With glassy eyes and degraded coordination, he pawed at the shrink wrap until it was mostly off. Then he tried to manhandle the seal on the box. Nothing doing. He tried to severe it with his fingernail. No go. One more attempt to pull it open and a few expletives later, Bookman's frustration overcame his good judgment and he weaved to the kitchen for a sharp knife to do in the obstinate obstacle. Jamming it into the breach he freed the captive DVD, but it also left a deep puncture wound on the heel of Bookman's left hand.

A few more expletives and a bandage later, Bookman managed with the required delicacy to place the disk in the tray and start up the movie. He left his kitchen looking like a crime scene.

Another pour he didn't know he was pouring, another pull he didn't know he was pulling, and this one longer than most as for some reason his hand seemed to be throbbing in pain. He looked down at it and remembered the knife incident and took another pull.

Bookman watched along for a while, getting the gist of it. At least they tell you right up front what this crap is all about. One guy: "The Secret gives you anything you want: happiness, health, and wealth." Another guy: "You can have, do, or be anything you want."

If that's true, Bookman thought, would that second guy choose to be that fat? Or that bald? I guess he didn't want those hair follicles enough.

You can have it all. Big house, big car, big bank account, and all you have to do is want it bad enough. You can be cured of any disease, loose the weight, get the girl, travel the world. This makes my skin crawl.

Another pour he didn't know he was pouring, another drink he didn't know he was drinking.

"The Secret is the law of attraction!" says another guy they're interviewing for this pseudo-documentary. A quote flashes up on the screen: "Everything that's coming into your life you are attracting into your life," it says. "And it's attracted to you by virtue of the images you're holding in your mind. It's what you're thinking.

Whatever is going on in your mind you are attracting to you."

So that's the game, is it? Thinks Bookman. Mind control, that's all it takes, eh?

"Thoughts become things."

From that point on, Bookman tuned out. The movie kept playing in front of him and he was in no mood to deal with the remote, so the disk kept spinning through different examples as to how this so-called law of attraction could draw wealth, health, relationships, youthful appearance and vigor, and general happiness anyone's way who set his or her mind to the task of imagining his or her universe.

In and out Bookman's mind went, the movie interspersed with bouts of seething anger, not just toward the movie but more often towards life in general.

> It's really important that you feel good, because this feeling good is what goes out as a signal into the Universe and starts to attract more of itself to you. So the more you can feel good, the more you will attract the things that help you feel good, and are able to keep bringing you up higher and higher.

Another pour he didn't know he was pouring, another drink he didn't know he was drinking.

> Marci Shimoff shared a wonderful quote from the great Albert Einstein: "The most important question any human being can ask themselves is, 'Is this a friendly Universe?'"

Gees, what is it with these people and Einstein? His theories have posed the single greatest threat to Catholicism of any scientist in history. They don't know what they're doing. They're playing with fire with that guy.

> You must believe that you have received. You must know that what you want is yours the moment you ask. You must have complete and utter faith.

That's exactly what Jesus said! They stole that from us!

But that's not what he meant, Bookman quickly backpedaled. He meant that in a spiritual sense...still, he did say it, Bookman argued with himself. Ah, shut the hell up! What the hell do you know anyway!

> It's the feeling that really creates the attraction, not just the picture or the thought. A lot of people think, "If I think positive thoughts, or if I visualize having what I want, that will be enough." But if you're doing that and still not feeling abundant, or feeling loving or joyful, then it doesn't create the power of attraction.

"Ah, what the hell does this guy know?" Bookman may have said out loud, very out loud. So now it was the feeling and not thoughts. Pretty soon they'll tell me it's something else. And then when you give it a try and it doesn't work—when life stays just the way it's always been—they tell you you're not holding your mouth right, or you don't have enough faith, or some other kind of crap. It's all just one big scam.

Another pour...another drink...

Bookman must have dozed off. When he came to, toward the end of the movie, a female narrator was saying:

> You are God in a physical body. You are Spirit in the flesh. You are Eternal Life expressing itself as You. You are cosmic being. You are all powerful. You are all wisdom. You are all intelligence. You are perfection. You are magnificence. You are the creator, and you are creating the creation of You on this planet.

"Blasphemy!" Bookman cried. "Blasphemy!" This is precisely what Satan was cast out of heaven for! Daring to be like God!

Bookman's anger quickly gave way to tears. He'd fallen asleep, hunched over in his chair. His back would hurt tomorrow and his hand was throbbing for some reason. He made the herculean effort to put the footrest up and push his seatback into recumbent mode.

When the movie was over, the screen reverted to the menu, over which pleasant New Age music played. To the soothing intonations, Bookman dreamed he was dying, a white light opened above him and he was completely at peace. At that moment, he felt at one with the light, infused by it. And he had to admit next morning when he woke up that it had felt pretty good.

"Get a load of this one, Bookman, from The Secret*:*

> *"When you are feeling good feelings, it is communication back from the Universe saying, 'You are thinking good thoughts.' Likewise, when you are feeling bad, you are receiving communications back from the Universe saying, 'You are thinking bad thoughts.'"*

Bookman just shook his head.

Chapter 12

"Are you sober today?" Bookman asked through the grate.

"Yes, my son," said Father Justin. "Tell me your sins, or your clues, as you prefer."

Bookman sat back, rubbed his neck. "Something a little out of the ordinary happened. I'm at odds to explain it. The books from this book club..."

"What about them?"

"They got me thinking, that's all." He looked down at his bandaged hand.

"Never a good thing. It's best to leave the thinking to the catechism. That's all the thinking we need to do."

"I gotta tell you, Justin," Bookman said. "Since that day with the Chief, some of this stuff rings true. I don't want it to, but it does. I would never tell anybody this except you."

"There's only one truth, John," Father Justin said. "It's the Catholic truth."

"What about what you were saying the other

day?"

"I was drunk. Who knows what I'm capable of saying when I'm drunk?"

"But that's the point, isn't it? This doesn't seem to be doing us any good. Why is that?"

"But what about the next life?" Father Justin said. "What happens then?"

Bookman squirmed. "Yeah, but maybe there's a way to accommodate both. Can't we mind our Ps and Qs about the Mass and the other sacraments *and* give something new a chance?"

"That's how it starts but where does it end?"

"Could it be worse than it is?"

"It could be a lot worse. You could end up in hell."

"Let me give you a for instance," Bookman said. "This fellow, we'll call him Jarmel. He follows a particular book called *Think and Grow Rich*. Have you heard of it?"

"No."

"He followed this book to the letter and in a weird way it worked out. Sure, he's in a body cast and he's going to have problems for the rest of his life, but it worked out."

"These things work out but they have terrible consequences, John. Isn't that the fact?"

"In his case, yes," Bookman said. "In his case, yes."

Bookman thought that through. The way that guy did it was strange, but he'd read through *Think and Grow Rich* early that morning and he couldn't discount something about the content of the book, something about its spirit.

"Is this all you have to go on?" Father Justin said. "For the case?"

"Just the books," Bookman said. "Something tells me Berg was right about them. What that something is, I don't know."

"The functioning of reason is a difficult subject for the Catholic," Father Justin said. "Look to Thomas Aquinas. The *Summa Theologica* is our guide on these matters. He brought it all together. A perfect fusion of Aristotle and faith. No need to go beyond Thomas. In fact, it's dangerous to do so. It's what the Catechism is based on. Just read your catechism if you're interested in these things. Otherwise, leave it to us priests."

Bookman had anticipated this advice. He'd also brushed up on the Catechism and Aquinas that morning. It had felt as dead as the other books felt alive to him.

"Dangerous?" Bookman said. "Why would it be dangerous?"

"Just trust me on this one, John," Father Justin said. "It's dangerous. You don't know what your getting yourself into. Leave it alone. Do you hear me? Just leave it alone."

"Fine," Bookman said. "It's dangerous." Bookman gave his friend a moment to calm down. "I think I like you better when you're drunk."

Bookman heard a snort. Father Justin had pulled himself together.

"So you want to tell my why this gets you going like this?"

"Is this my confession or yours?" Father Justin

asked. "It gets me going, as you say, because if Aquinas is wrong, Catholicism as we know it is too."

* * *

Outside on the street, his finger still wet with holy water, Bookman turned his cell phone on. He'd missed a call from Berg. He hit the re-dial button.

"It's Bookman," he said.

Berg: "Susan Ross is back in town."

"Who's Susan Ross?"

"*Zen and the Art of Motorcycle Maintenance.* She's been hiking in the Himalayas."

"That's a pretty short trip," Bookman said. "Pick me up."

* * *

"They said I went hiking in the Himalayas?"

"That's what they said," Berg confirmed.

"Who said that?"

He flipped through his wheelbook but found no annotation. "I think it was Todd Gack."

Susan Ross let out an incredulous puff of breath. "How would he know?" she said.

"It was corroborated by Steve Genderson," Bookman said.

"Oh," Ross said. "Well, I guess I haven't kept people up to date on my movements. I was going to hike in Nepal but changed my mind."

They met at a downtown diner. It was a favorite for interviews because it put people at ease and there was a quiet booth in the back where not much could be heard over the low din of other customers and the whisper of radio from the cash register at the other end of the place.

"So you know Steve Genderson," Berg said.

"Yes," she said. "I know him very well." There was something enigmatic in the response. "What's this all about anyway?"

"Sue Ellen Pinkus was murdered," Berg said.

"Oh." Susan Ross's eyes were wide. "Wow."

"The day before you left town," Bookman added.

"Wow." She hadn't heard him, still processing the fact of the death. She opened her bag and took out a pack of cigarettes.

"I'm afraid you can't smoke in here, Ms. Ross," Berg said.

"I'm sitting here with two policemen who've just told me a friend of mine was murdered," she said. "Arrest me if you want to." She took a long draw and let it out to the side. After a moment, she said, "If it offends you, I'll put it out."

Both detectives shook their heads.

She said, "You know what? Maybe we should do this another time."

"Just a couple of questions," Berg said. "What was the nature of your relationship with the victim?"

"I've known Sue Ellen a long time," she said. "We grew up together and when my mom died, her parents more or less took me in. Not literally in. I lived officially with my aunt, but..."

"I'm sorry," Berg said. "We had no idea you were so close."

"If you weren't in the Himalayas," Bookman said. "Where were you?"

"I was hiking a stretch of the Appalachian trail instead," she answered. "With a friend."

"Does this friend have a name?" Bookman said.

"Yes."

Bookman and Berg waited until wordlessly she gave up opposition to this invasion of privacy.

"His name is Wyck Thayer," she said. "I guess he's my boyfriend now."

"And what about Steve Genderson?" Bookman pursued.

"What does this have to do with anything?" Ross asked.

"We're just trying to get the lay of the land, that's all," soothed Berg.

"He's a really good broker. Honest. When my mom died she had a pretty sizable life insurance policy and left the money to me. You probably already know I'm meeting with him in a couple of days."

"We didn't know that, actually," Berg said.

She was looking down now, her brown hair shielding her face, out of which passed a curl of smoke. "He says he has a business proposition to discuss."

"What sort of business proposition?" Bookman asked.

"I don't know. Probably some sort of stock of-fering or something."

Berg looked at Bookman. Given Ross's re-action—there was real pain in her face—this interrogation was already running long. "Just one more question, Ms. Ross," he said.

"Shoot."

"It's about the book you wanted to present to Todd Gack's book club," he said.

"*Zen and the Art of Motorcycle Maintenance*? What about it?"

"Gack shot it down," Berg said, trying to get her talking.

"He said it was a book of philosophy and not a self-improvement book per se," she said. "Fair enough."

"So you quit the group over it?" Bookman said.

"When my mom died I read all those books and a few more. If I'd wanted to stay in the group I would have picked another one."

"So why'd you quit?" Berg asked.

"I don't know that I quit. I wasn't really ever a part of it."

Again, the detectives waited.

"I never really got on with Gack," she finally said.

"Even though your close friend was seeing him?" Bookman asked.

"It was an issue, ok?"

Bookman: "How much of an issue?"

"Enough of an issue that I didn't want to be in the book club," she said. "It was as much Sue Ellen's as it was his. For whatever personal insecurity Gack had about it, he says keep out *Zen and the Art*—which is a pivotal book, it brings all these other books together—and they keep it out. She took his side. It was an issue. It was a big issue. Gack has this idea that Eckhart Tolle is the end-all-be-all in self-improvement literature. He put the group together basically to prove everybody else wrong and himself and Tolle right. I guess he saw *Zen and the Art* as a real threat to that goal of his."

"That seems odd," Berg said.

"Gack thinks he gets it but he doesn't get it at all."

"And you do?" Bookman said.

"When my mom died, I was crushed. I dropped everything and started reading, searching. Then one day something cracked. It had the sound of ice cracking on a frozen pond. I'll never forget that moment."

"Yes," said Bookman. It was an involuntary reaction to what Ross had just said, and it came from deep down inside. This was what he had experienced in Chief Farkus's office that day. It hadn't been ice for him, more like an eggshell, a very thick eggshell but an eggshell nonetheless, the lone fissure betraying the fragility of this seemingly impenetrable structure that had protected him for so many years.

When both Berg and Ross looked at him, he apologized. "Please...go on."

"I think I know what you're talking about," Berg said. "But we're looking at all these books and I have to say I'm not quite putting it all together."

"And you want me to break it down for you?" Ross said. "Here? Right now?"

"I understand this is a bad time for you," Berg said, but he left his thought unfinished.

First Susan Ross's shoulders slumped. Then she reconciled herself to the idea and lit up another cigarette.

She took a long draw, held it and then pushed it out. "First, you have these broad-based books that are supposed to generally improve your life: *As a Man Thinketh*, *Your Erroneous Zones, Don't Sweat the Small Stuff, Seven Habits, How to Win Friends*. What do all of these have in common? Thinking. It's the power of the mind that brings everything to you. Just change the way you think about things. Stop looking at a problem as a problem and it ceases to be a problem. Dr. Covey, Wayne Dyer and all these others are probably 'enlightened' people themselves, and they're trying to think their way through what that means, studying various enlightened and successful people and translating that into words.

"Covey had a spiritual awakening and he's trying to describe it from one mind to the next, from his mind to yours. Same with Dale Carnegie. Mr. Carnegie was probably a highly evolved, enlightened person. What he is describing is the surface layer of an enlightened person's life, what he does, how he behaves in various situations. If you want to see model behavior of an enlightened person, read that book."

"*How to Win Friends*," Berg offered.

"Right," Ross said. "He's describing it. Problem is, he's describing it to unenlightened minds, minds that haven't experienced the awakening yet. They can't apply what they're reading consistently even if they want to. And he doesn't tell them how to make that awakening happen

119

either. No one can. That's why they say it requires a divine touch.

"Then Tolle comes along and he provides a lot of useful additional information. He talks about the need for awakening to take place. He talks about dis-identification from the mind. He talks about becoming the watcher of your own mind. Listen, he says, to your own internal monologue."

"Gack talked about that," Berg said, breaking in.

"What is that voice in your head saying?" Ross continued unperturbed. "Does it make sense? Is it negative? Is it mired in the past? Does it have any consistent themes? Don't do anything about it. Allow it to be, but observe. Then he asks, 'Ok, who are you? The voice, the internal monologue? Or the one listening to it? Become the listener. This is who you are. The other is the ego and is not you. Allow it to be, watch it, observe it and it will dissipate and eventually disappear, leaving you as the divine presence that you are.'"

"Buddhism," Bookman said.

"Not Buddhism," Ross said. "A principle of Buddhism, of the Buddha. And also of the Christ, if you're willing to look closely enough. 'Consider the lilies of the field...' Enlightened thought. And of Judaism: 'The Lord is my shepherd, I shall not want.' Enlightened thinking. Sufism, a branch of Islam, is all about enlightenment too."

"Interesting," Berg said.

"The most famous awakening, probably, is Paul

on the road to Damascus. He had a crisis, followed by a visit from a spiritual teacher. That's the pattern. Who knows, maybe one of you is becoming enlightened. You've now been visited by Tolle."

Both Berg and Bookman looked at their hands, afraid to catch anyone's eye. There was an observed moment of silence, during which only Ross made a sound, drawing in, blowing out, stubbing out, lighting up.

"Where does the 'power of now' come in?" Berg asked.

"The concept? Or the book?" When Berg hesitated, Ross plowed ahead: "You can only observe the internal monologue if you're present in the moment. And if you notice, the internal monologue is always focused somewhere else, either in the past of in the future. There aren't any problems 'right now,' only in the past and in the future. Think about it." She pointed in the detectives' direction with the new cigarette perched between index and middle finger. "There is never, ever a problem right now."

Berg bobbed his head a little in agreement.

"My friend is dead. You have a case to solve. But right now, at this moment, that's just the way it is. Facts, not problems. I feel the pain of it in my physical being. Right here," she said, pointing to her heart. "It's a physical sensation. An emotion, which is the body's physical reaction to a thought. In this case a sad, sad thought."

"We can do this some other time," Berg said.

"No, this is good, actually," Ross said. "Let's keep going. That's the thing, you know. That sensation isn't going to kill me. And it isn't who I am. It's *in* me, for sure, but it doesn't take me over. Nothing does anymore. Who I am is this background presence, this space where this sadness is allowed to be. Does that make sense to you?"

"I think so," Berg said.

Bookman begrudged her a terse nod to get her to go on with her story. The physical sensation *he* was feeling was of fear that he might actually be falling for this story of one who very well could be the killer.

"This background presence has power over the mind to change it. Otherwise, you're working with the source of the problem, the mind, to try to solve the problem—also the mind. But the mind has no power to overcome itself. It has no leverage. If you are your mind, you're locked in. See what I mean?"

This time, Berg's nod was polite but non-committal.

"The million-dollar question remains *how* to awaken," she went on. "Even Tolle can't tell us that. Here..." She reached into her purse and pulled out a Kindle e-book reader. "I've marked the place where he says..."

"You have all the books right there?" Berg said, impressed, remembering the stack that walled in his desk like sandbags around a foxhole.

She punched a few buttons. "Here it is. Page 117, *A New Earth*:

"[T]here is nothing you can do to become free of the ego. When that shift happens, which is the shift from thinking to awareness, an intelligence far greater than the ego's cleverness begins to operate in your life.

"Yes, yes," Berg said. "I read that one to you, Bookman. Remember?"

"It's a shift that happens spontaneously at some point," Ross went on. "A paradigm shift, but not the mental shift from personality ethic to character ethic that Covey talks about, though that will inevitably happen too. Tolle is talking about 'a shift from thinking to awareness,' from the 'ego's cleverness' to the far superior intelligence of presence."

"Presence, huh?" Berg said.

"He also says somewhere else, though, that it's only the first spark that happens by divine intervention, so to speak. Once that happens, it can't be stopped. Once you start to see the illusion as illusion, you can't revert back. The whole process can be 'delayed by the ego,' however. Maybe indefinitely, who knows?"

Delayed by the ego, Bookman repeated to himself. This had something to do with the case, he was sure of it.

She put down the Kindle. "As I describe it to you, it seems as plain as the nose on your face, but some get it, some don't. Some will do it, some won't. Only when the pain gets to be so intense that you simply drop all pretense does the illusion start to go away, does the paradigm shift."

"Suffering," Bookman said.

"Suffering," Ross agreed. "But conscious suffering. You have to make it conscious before it starts to burn away the ego."

"Can I take a look at that thing?" Berg asked, pointing to the Kindle.

"Sure," Ross said.

Bookman looked at Berg as he fiddled with the gadget and remembered watching the pain his partner had gone through in the divorce. Bookman remembered his own divorce too so many years before and how he had "borne the burden of it," gotten through it with a bottle of bourbon and had come out of it with only a bad habit to show for his troubles. (This was what Bookman told himself, though his addiction had begun many years before and had been part of the reason for the demise of his marriage; after the divorce his drinking had simply gotten worse—it became more entrenched, steadier and in actuality more livable, at least now that he was alone.) Maybe I've missed my chance to allow the pain to crush me, Bookman thought. Maybe I would have been better off if I'd had a nervous breakdown.

In truth, Susan Ross was describing precisely what had occurred in Chief Farkus's office, but Bookman couldn't quite get his mind around that connection just yet.

"But Jesus did say, 'Seek and ye shall find,'" Ross said. "So in that sense, maybe we all do hold the power to get that transcendental ball rolling, after all. It's a mystery, I guess."

"What about Scott Drake?" Bookman asked.

"Sue Ellen wasn't serious about him," Ross said. "She hooked up with him just to make Gack jealous."

"Maybe it worked," Bookman said.

Ross's pale skin went noticeably whiter, unable to muster any ire. "They had a weird thing between them, she and Gack, that's for sure."

"What about Drake?" Bookman asked. "People don't generally like to be used in that way."

"No," Ross objected. "That kid kind of gets it. He wouldn't do anything like this."

"Kid?" Bookman repeated. "How old are you?"

"I'm 27," Ross said. "Surely you realize by now, Detective, everyone is a kid to me. I suppose at some point you're going to tell me how she died."

"She was shot through the neck," Bookman said.

Ross hung her head again, just as Berg held out the Kindle. When he hesitated, she said, "What is it?"

"How does this fit in?" Berg asked. He'd manage to find in the device the cover of *Zen and the Art of Motorcycle Maintenance.*

"It doesn't," Ross said. "It's a book of philosophy."

"So Gack was right," Bookman said.

"But it does show the difference between the two." When they looked at her blankly, she said, "The mind-led individual and the spirit-led individual." Blank stares. "The ancient philosophical conspiracy? Aristotle? Ever heard of him?"

"I've heard of him," Berg said, shrugging. "But—"

"In the Aristotelian framework, the world was no longer governed first and foremost by a belief in the unmanifested world. The discovery of truth in the *material* world became the governing principle in the thimble full of minds that really mattered, society's elite. And that mindset since the Renaissance has gradually taken root and displaced the mindset based on 'the Good' or as Persig puts it in *Zen and the Art*, 'Quality,' in modern society. But 'at what cost?' as he says."

"What is all this?" Bookman said.

"You've lost me," agreed Berg.

"Yeah," Ross said, taking a puff. "Maybe we should start at the beginning. Let me see," she said, looking at the Kindle, pressing some of its buttons, the cigarette hanging from her lips. "Here. Here's the beginning." She read a sentence or two to herself.

"Ok," she said. "Before Socrates, the Greek mind was ruled by a concept called *arête*. *Arête* meant a duty of excellence to oneself. Excellence was the highest goal, a harmony inside and out, determined through direct interaction with reality.

"*Arête* to the Greeks of Homer's time, 400 years before Socrates, was all-encompassing. Persig puts it this way: '[*Arête*] was not a form of reality. It was reality itself, ever changing, ultimately unknowable in any kind of fixed, rigid way.'"

"Ok," Berg said.

"*Arête* was a qualitative measure of man's interaction with his world, with his reality. The end goal of his philosophy was how well he interacted with his environment. Plato changed all of that by placing the 'True' at the head of the table where *arête* used to sit."

"Why is that important?" Berg asked.

"It's important because it determines how we decide what to do. If *arête* is the highest goal, then every decision we make is designed to ensure harmony inside ourselves and in the world around us; it requires complete and utter present-moment consciousness as a part of our decision-making process at all times. How we feel from moment to moment and our impact on our world is of the utmost importance."

"Ok."

"If the True is the highest goal, we are engaged in a theoretical discussion based on judgment in which reality plays only a limited role; it requires no self-consciousness whatsoever. All negativity—war, violence, hatred—arises from unconsciousness."

"That's an interesting perspective," Berg said.

"*Arête* is another word for consciousness."

"Here we go," Bookman muttered.

"It's important to understand exactly how Plato went about selling this new scheme to the people of his day," Ross continued. "If you can understand this history, you'll understand why we think the way we do and what needs to be done to solve the problems of the modern world."

"Oh, I gotta hear this," Bookman said.

"First, Plato made up out of whole cloth the world of ideas."

"Plato made up ideas?" Berg clarified.

Bookman: "For crying out loud."

"He did," Ross confirmed. "It's hard for us to imagine now that looking at the world in terms of ideas is not part of reality, but it isn't. It's a fiction, made up by Plato, a construction he thought would help us understand reality better, but it's not reality itself. Ideas require judgment of reality, and limit direct experience of reality."

"I think I get what you mean," Berg said, while Bookman continued to shake his head.

"To go along with ideas, Plato said there were also Appearances. Ideas were changeless, while Appearances were constantly changing. Thus, for example, we have the Idea of a horse, which never changes, and we also have the Appearance of a particular horse, which undergoes constant change. Plato's famous 'horse versus horseness' dichotomy."

"Right," Berg said. "Right. That...old thing."

"Neither Ideas nor Appearances has anything to do with reality. It's all in the head."

"So where does *arête* fit into Plato's scheme, according to this Persig?" Bookman asked.

"That's the important part," Ross explained. "Plato put it under the Idea heading. In essence, he took *arête*, which he called 'the Good,' and placed it as the highest among the Ideas."

"God," Bookman said. "He put God at the top, in other words. That sounds pretty good to me."

"Well, no," Ross said. "Not exactly. As I said, *arête* to the Greeks pre-Socrates was a quailtative measure of man's interaction with his world, with his reality. The end goal of his philosophy was how well he interacted with his environment. But it wasn't an idea at all. It *was* reality."

"'In him we live and move and have our being,'" Bookman said. He was uncomfortable with the quotation from the Bible, always had been. What Ross had called Plato's position seemed right to him before, but now he wasn't so sure of himself.

"Very good, Detective," Ross said. "You're starting to connect the dots. That's St. Paul you just quoted. And do you know where he said that?"

Bookman couldn't recall.

"He said that in Athens to the philosophers in the Areopagus, the same city where the philosophical drama we're talking about now unfolded. Paul's conversion, in fact, was a conversion from Aristotelianism back to this pre-Socratic understanding of existence we're talking about now. He was trying to tell the philosophers of Athens where they had gone wrong."

"Wow," Berg said. "You really did read every-thing."

"But I'm getting ahead of myself," Ross said. "Plato was developing his whole scheme—Ideas and Appearances—in an effort to get at the Truth. The Truth was Plato's highest ideal, not *arête*, the harmonious interaction with reality. The pursuit of truth has nothing whatsoever to do with reality. It's a theoretical construction. It's a conversation one has in the mind. Forget about reality, in other words, don't worry about internal and external harmony. Root yourself in theory, in ideas, which are simply constructions of the mind.

"And now that the Good is merely an idea, it too is devoid of any contact with reality. What is Good and what is not Good is simply a theoretical discussion, not something that we glean and absorb from interaction with reality, with *arête*."

"With God," Bookman said.

"That's another way of putting it."

"So Plato was the bad guy," Berg said.

"No," Ross said. "He was 'hoisted with his own petard.'"

"Shakespeare," chirped Bookman.

"At least for Plato, the Good was the most important question of all. In other words, he was trying to get at what was True so he could figure out what was Good. That wasn't the case with his student, Aristotle. He didn't give a rat's ass what was Good. Consequently, he demoted the Good as far down the hierarchy of ideas as he could get away with, changing its name to Ethics, an afterthought in the world of Aristotelian science today."

"Wow," Berg said.

"Aristotle also tweaked Plato's concept of Appearances, creating a concept he called 'substance,' which was the underlying stuff to which the Appearances clung. He said that this 'substance' was just as unchanging as ideas were, and thus was an equally valid subject of study. And he set the educated world willy-nilly to the task of collection of facts concerning substance. This we call science today and the philosophy Aristotle created thereby we call materialism.

"And the once-proud *arête*—or God, or reality, call it what you like—he devolved into a completely separate study called Metaphysics (and later came theology), while science barrels on alone, determining what's True, limiting its field of inquiry to this stuff called substance, devoid of any meaning or context."

The detectives sat mute, unable to process what had just been explained to them.

"Don't you see what's happened here?" Ross said.

"No," Bookman said.

"No," Berg agreed.

"What is it detectives say?" Ross lowered her voice to a masculine pitch: "'Just the facts, ma'am.'"

Berg smiled.

"What does that have to do with anything?" Bookman asked.

"It has everything to do with the history I've just explained to you. Now you have science, the facts, as all important, with ethics, the Good, as an unimportant footnote. You've turned God into and idea and then basically dispensed with that idea. You've demoted God out of existence."

"All you've done is describe the way the modern world has systematically eliminated God from public discourse," Bookman said.

"Precisely," Ross said. "But without the illusion of a cohesive philosophy, good people would never have done that. For centuries now, we've been taught that this is the only coherent way to think. But it isn't. Materialism is a faith just like Christianity or Islam. Any theory of the nature of reality must necessarily be a faith because we're a part of reality."

"I'm afraid I still don't get it," Berg said.

"Are you a religious man, Detective Berg?" Ross asked.

Berg's answer came out as an admission. "No," he said sitting back. A half-smile had formed.

"Your friend here has that on you," Ross said. "As a religious man, he has one foot in the Aristotelian camp and one in the pre-Socratic camp. While that puts him at odds with himself, making him completely conflicted and unhappy, it also gives him some reference point toward understanding what Persig is talking about."

"I understand it but I don't agree with it," Bookman said.

"Your mind is firmly established, Detective Berg, in the modern mindset that Aristotle made up for us," Ross said, ignoring Bookman's comment. "It's a mythology—your mythology—just like the Christian mythology it has now replaced."

"The jury's still out on that one, sister," Bookman said.

"I'm sorry," Berg said. "I'm just not following what you mean."

"I know," Ross said. "I know." She took a long drag, pushed it out. "Pre-Socrates humans, and most people in the Middle Ages and some people today don't live in a world one step removed from reality, deadened by a layer of ideas or analytical thought like most of us in the mechanized world do today. They were and are one with reality. The world of ideas is merely an invention."

"Are you trying to tell us that Socrates made all this up and then convinced everybody to approach life this way?" Bookman argued.

"He didn't make it up," Ross said. "It was already a part of humanity long before Socrates came along. He just encouraged it, he gave it legitimacy. Guys like Siddhãrtha Gautama, better known as the Buddha, who was before Socrates, already understood the problem. And then Jesus, better known as the Christ, came along to preach specifically against what had become the de facto religion of his day, Aristotelianism. Socrates won out in the West and Buddha won out in the East, at least until recently. The Aristotelian cancer has spread to virtually the whole world at this point. Who knows what will happen when it takes over completely? Maybe Universal Intelligence will flip the switch on the sun and start over in some other corner of the cosmos."

Berg shook his head hopelessly.

"I know," Ross repeated. "You're not going to get it because that's the mythos you live in. You think your mental reconstruction of the world is real, but it isn't. Your only hope is to meditate on it. That's how it will come to you."

Berg shook his head again.

"You don't get that either," Ross said. "Do you?

Meditation. That's exactly the issue we're talking about. It just doesn't compute for you, the modern man."

"Surely you give credit to Aristotle for the advances of science," Bookman said.

"Not really," Ross said. "There's a much better way to think. That's what the first half of this book is all about," she said pointing to the Kindle, which still showed the front page of *Zen and the Art of Motorcycle Maintenance.*

"Bookman, here's something from The Seven Habits:

> "I am persuaded that many of the principles embodied in the Seven Habits are already deep within us, in our conscience and in our common sense. To recognize and develop them and to use them in meeting our deepest concerns, we need to think differently, to shift our paradigms to a new, deeper, inside-out level."

"Fascinating," Bookman grumbled.

Chapter 13

"According to Persig," Ross said, "if Socrates, Plato and Aristotle had not been rediscovered during the Renaissance, we'd still be living in caves."

"That's what I'm talking about," Bookman said.

"What you've been describing doesn't seem like so much to give up for all we've gotten," Berg said.

"But he also quotes Thoreau: 'You never gain something but that you lose something.'"

"And just what did we lose?" Bookman challenged.

"We can fly to the moon and back but we can't live with ourselves."

"Oh, right," Berg said.

"Aristotelian science leads only to progress for progress's sake. We're all still going to die. We are no closer to understanding the nature of reality and where it came from. Aristotelian science just can't answer these questions. It doesn't have the vocabulary for it. By chasing endlessly after facts, new theories, new hypotheses, with no direction in terms of value, science isn't producing more clarity, it's producing *less* clarity, a far cry from the brave new world it has always promised. Aristotelianism only causes chaos," Ross said. "There's a much better way to think."

"And what is this way?" Bookman asked. "According to you."

Ross said, "Quality."

"Quality is this better way of thinking?" Bookman said.

"That's what Persig calls it. Quality is man's direct interface with reality, as opposed to remaining one step removed from reality in the world of ideas. One might also call it *arête*, or God. When you remove the screen of ideas, you are in direct contact with God, the source of all understanding. Of course you're going to be better able to fix the motorcycle at that point."

"You may have a point," Berg said.

"In a different place he says this along the same lines:

> "The formation of hypotheses is the most mysterious of all the categories of scientific method. Where they come from, no one knows. A person is sitting somewhere, minding his own business, and suddenly...flash!...he understands something he didn't understand before. Until it's tested the hypothesis isn't truth. For the tests aren't its source. Its source is somewhere else."

"I quoted that to the boss!" Berg said. "Remember that, Bookman?"

"Congratulations," Bookman said.

"And there was that other one from Tolle," Berg said, excited. "What was it…"

"That's right," Ross said.

"It was weird, you know," Berg said. "I was just reading that in one book and then I switched to the other book, you know. And then the Chief called us in and it just came to me that the two were saying the same thing and that it applied to what the Chief was saying. Wow! That's so interesting."

"It is," Ross said. "That's exactly the point of it."

Berg pointed to the Kindle. "You have the Tolle books in there too, right?"

"I do," Ross said. After a few clicks she read:

> "The surprising result of a nationwide inquiry among America's most imminent mathematicians, including Einstein, to find out their working methods, was that thinking plays only a subordinate part in the brief, decisive phase of the creative act."

"Yes, that's the one," Berg said.

"Imagine a whole world of scientists who think like Einstein did," Ross said. "The *Tao te Ching* says something similar. It says, 'A good scientist has freed himself of concepts and keeps his mind open to what is.' Something like that. Hypotheses come to us from the unmanifested and bubble up into our consciousness. Aristotle thought it was the other way around, that we relate to reality through our minds. The better way to think is to realize the source of all wisdom and understanding and it isn't our brains."

"'The fear of God is the beginning of wisdom,'" Bookman quoted from the Bible.

"Exactly," Ross said, pointing her cigarette at Bookman. "It's the difference between thinking and meditating. What you didn't understand a few minutes ago."

"I think I get it now," Berg said.

"Yes, maybe you do," Ross said.

Looking at Bookman, Berg said, "We've kind of come full circle, haven't we?"

"'We've kind of come full circle, haven't we?'" Bookman repeated in a childish voice. "This is just some guy's brainchild. The Catholic Church has had all this worked out for a thousand years. I think I'll stick with Aquinas, if you don't mind."

"The one that brought Aristotle into the church," Ross said. "*Summa Theologica?*"

"You've heard of it," Bookman said. "Very impressive."

"Would it surprise you that Socrates himself was well aware of Persig's criticism?"

"Since they lived more than two thousand years apart, yes," Bookman said.

"Let me read you something from Plato's *Phaedo.* This is Socrates speaking:

"I am very far from admitting that he who contemplates existence through the medium of ideas sees them only 'through a glass darkly,' any more than he who sees them in their working and effects."

Bookman's face went ashen and he bent forward a little as if stricken by an imaginary blow. A groan was barely audible but Berg picked up on it. As a first-rate detective, even Bookman had to admit, if only to himself, that he'd just been fingered. If he were a character in an Agatha Christie novel, this would be the point in the proceedings when, with all the other suspects gathered around, the uniformed police officer would come to put him in handcuffs and take him away.

"What is it?" Berg said, looking from Ross to Bookman.

When Bookman didn't respond at the appropriate interval, Ross said, "I think your friend here has just had a very sudden insight, what James Joyce might have called an epiphany. One he's none too happy to have."

Bookman heard what Ross was saying but it was as one sick in bed with a fever, his sainted mother coming in and out of his room, placing a cold washcloth on his forehead. She is talking but he can't hear her over the sound of blood flowing through his ears. Bookman felt a sudden craving for a drink. An onslaught. His mouth went dry, but so was his coffee cup.

"I don't get it," he hears Berg saying.

Ross says, "Saint Paul uses this exact phrase in one of the most famous passages in the Bible. It's called the Love Chapter."

Bookman knew the passage well. His Protestant father, may he rest in peace, helped him memorize it when he was a boy. The Prods were big on that one and big on memorization. He quoted it in his mind:

> For we know in part, and we prophesy in part.

> But when that which is perfect is come, then that which is in part shall be done away.

> When I was a child, I spake as a child, I understood as a child, I thought as a child: but when I became a man, I put away childish things.

Picking up where Bookman's memory trailed away, Ross said, "Give me a sec and I'll read it to you...here:

> For now we see through a glass, darkly; but then face to face: now I know in part; but then shall I know even as also I am known."

Through a glass, darkly. The phrase was unmistakable and haunting. There was no denying from whence Paul had lifted it. Bookman silently finished the passage: "And now abideth faith, hope, charity, these three; but the greatest of these is charity."

"Whereas Plato and Socrates wouldn't admit that filtering the world through a mentally-constructed screen of ideas leaves us one step removed from reality, Paul, one of the founders of Christianity, argues the contrary to a Hellenized world."

"He's calling them back to this *areté* you've been talking about," Berg said.

"Or non-dualism, as people call it these days.

Most people think Paul is referring here to the next life, but he isn't. He's talking about the real world, uncluttered by its false mock up of ideas. He isn't talking about heaven, he's talking about the paradigm shift, the shift from unconsciousness to consciousness, awakening, enlightenment—salvation, not in some future heaven, but now. Paul was an educated man. He would have been well-acquainted with Socrates, Plato and Aristotle. He didn't use this famous phrase by accident."

"Interesting," Berg said. He looked at Bookman, who was clearly agitated. His mind was somewhere else. "Interesting stuff," Berg said to fill the silent gap.

Bookman was busy acclimating himself to his new worldview. He suddenly saw his beloved Church objectively for what it was. The identification was broken, and disorientingly so. Realities he refused even to entertain before were no longer anathema.

Why, for example, weren't the percentages of decent people inside the Church even slightly better than outside the Church—truth be told, the data were skewed in the opposite direction. It seemed the evidence—anecdotal though it was—should have been clearly the opposite if the "salvation" offered there was worth a damn.

And why was it of such primal importance that he come to a conclusion about historical figures and events for which he could not possibly have sufficient data to reach those conclusions? Was Jesus God? Did he rise from the dead? Did he ascend into heaven? How the hell did he know? And of what possible concern could Bookman's opinion—about *anything*—be to the Deity? This was all just silliness to obfuscate the real problem: that the priests didn't know what the hell they were talking about anymore, they'd lost their way entirely.

And then, of course, there was his and Justin's drinking problem. No one practiced Catholicism harder than they did, no one was more pure in his observance of the sacraments. Another quote from St. Paul came to mind: "a Pharisee among Pharisees."

"Yeah," Ross said. She picked up the Kindle and clicked back to *Zen and the Art* and looked at it mistily. "This is the book that started it all for me. What it represents is a rational philosophical defense of 'The Now,' as Tolle puts it. In the Now is where we meet God, in other words. If the present moment is the only one that exists, that means the future is totally dependent upon the present moment for its existence. This opens the door for books like *The Secret*. Who's to say? It makes sense in a way."

"Yes, I sort of see what you mean," Berg said.

"I remember the first time I read this book, one passage about a train rolling down the tracks in particular. I had never heard of The Now, so I didn't associate it with that at the time. I got the impression as I read of being a train going along through my own reality and drawing up with each new moment the physical reality that surrounded me: passing houses, buildings, trees and lakes, a veritable Potemkin Village of reality. I was no longer a passive observer in creation, I was a participant in it. That vision has never left me. That's the vision of reality that this book conjures."

That speech was out of character with all she'd said before. There was a passion in it as if momentarily she had forgotten about her dead friend. Berg noticed the difference.

"That's very well said," he commented.

"It's something I've said before, many times, to many others. But not for a long time. Want the sound byte version? Here it is: 'The Quality which creates the world emerges as a relationship between man and his experience. He is a participant in the creation of all things.' That's *The Secret* in a nutshell, if you ask me."

"I think I'm catching on," Berg said.

"Tolle says exactly the same thing in *The Power of Now*. He says, '[Y]our perception of the world is a reflection of your state of consciousness.'"

"That's an interesting way of putting it," Berg said.

"Tolle also describes how modern physics has discovered that results of scientific experiments vary depending upon who is doing the experimentation. He says that the 'observing consciousness cannot be separated from the observed phenomena.' There appears to be no subject-object differentiation. Aristotle's 'substance' is not so unchanging as he thought. Science, itself, is beginning to prove Aristotle wrong, in other words."

"Interesting," Berg said.

"Who knows," said Ross. "Maybe string theory and chaos theory and even global warming are jokes that scientists have come up with and all it takes is enough people to believe in them for them to be true. Maybe that's how it works. Maybe it isn't theories describing reality; maybe it's reality adhering to theories. With enough faith you can do anything."

"Even move mountains," Bookman said. Berg and Ross looked at him as if he had just come out of a hypnotic trance.

"Just like Jesus said," Ross agreed. "Maybe he meant literally what he was saying. So maybe *The Secret* is right. The *Tao te Ching* says you can use the Tao any way you choose."

"Sounds more like religion to me," Bookman said.

"'In the temple of science, there are many mansions,'" Ross relied. "Albert Einstein, 1918. It's in the book." She held up the Kindle, then twisted her arm at the elbow to look at her watch. "I gotta go."

"But what about the books?" Berg said.

"What about them?"

"You were telling us all this to explain about the books," Berg said.

"Oh, right," Ross said. "It's simple. Some of the books—*How to Win Friends and Influence People*, *The Seven Habits*, *Don't Sweat the Small Stuff*— are Aristotelian. They try to solve the problems the mind has created with recourse to the mind. They're about thinking as opposed to being.

Some of them—*The Secret*, Tolle*, Zen and the Art*—are pre-Socratic. They stress being over thinking. They take a spiritual approach to solving the problems of the mind.

"And let me just say, it can be very frustrating to be told what you should do and then be unable to carry that out, which is where the Aristotelians find themselves. Without the paradigm shift—awakening—it's almost impossible to put any of this stuff into practice consistently. That's the position these people find themselves in, and when they're put in with a bunch of people who understand *arête*...let's just say it isn't a good situation."

"That would tend to rule out Gack," Berg said, looking to Bookman for confirmation.

"Well..." Ross said, reluctant to agree but unable to deny the implication.

"There's just one problem with your theory of the case," Bookman said, standing up.

"I wasn't aware I had a theory of the case, but—"

"You're forgetting, Ms. Ross, that Sue Ellen Pinkus's chosen book was *The Power of Positive Thinking*," Bookman said, stressing the word "Thinking" triumphantly. "Come on, Detective Berg. We've heard enough."

Ross stood up too, unperturbed, and collected her Kindle, dropping it into her bag.

"You've read *The Power of Positive Thinking*?" Ross said.

"As a matter of fact, I have," Bookman said.

"Then you know that it has very little to do with

thinking," she said. "Just like *Think and Grow Rich* has nothing to do with thinking and very little to do with growing rich."

"Those are pre-Socratic as well?" Berg said.

"You can't judge a book by its title," Ross said, stubbing out her last cigarette.

"And you should stop smoking," Bookman said, unable to muster anything more scathing.

"Why?" Ross said. "Smoking is a pleasure. I enjoy it."

"Maybe you'll enjoy lung cancer too," Bookman said. "The way you're sucking them down, that's where you're headed."

"Do you realize that I'm much more likely not to get cancer than I am to get it? Think about that. Why might that be if smoking is so bad for you? If that's how the world works—cold and mechanical?"

Berg started to say, "Statistically—"

"Here's a statistic for you: when they started to put those warning labels on cigarettes, smoking went down, but among those who continued to smoke, the incidence of cancer and smoking related illnesses went up. Why might that be? Could it be because the smokers started to believe it a little more?"

"Is that true?" Berg said.

"There's no study that backs that up," Bookman scoffed.

"Call it a hypothesis," Ross said. "It's how we know things. And besides, I'm not that attached to this life anyway."

* * *

"Check this out, Bookman:

*"In an article in Bits and Pieces, some sug-
gestions are made on how to keep a
disagreement from becoming an argument:
[For example] Welcome the disagreement.
Remember the slogan, 'When two partners
always agree, one of them is not necessary.'*

"That's from How to Win Friends."

*Bookman looked at Berg over his glasses. "I'm
starting to think that one partner is unnecessary,
indeed."*

Chapter 14

"Did you see what I saw in there?" Bookman
asked Berg once they reached the privacy of
their unmarked Crown Victoria.

"What's that?" Berg said.

"A person with that kind of philosophy lacks
any type of moral constraint. That's what we call
a sociopath in our business."

"You're crazy, Bookman."

"You heard her yourself. She said she answers
to nobody. No religion. Above religion."

"She's the opposite of a sociopath and you
know it, Bookman. You're just upset because
you couldn't rattle her, and she put it to Catholicism and you couldn't come up with an answer.
That's what's really going on here."

"No belief in guilt," Bookman said. "That's
exactly why I tried to rattle her, as you say. To
prove the point."

"There's no way that girl did it and you know

it."

"I don't know anything of the sort!" Bookman said.

"Fine. That's just fine." Berg wouldn't take the bait. He had other things on his mind. Susan Ross was still sitting in her car on the other side of the small parking lot. She'd made a call on her cell phone, head down most of the time. Both Bookman and Berg knew what that call was all about. They could feel the emotion of it across the short distance and through two panes of glass. Now she was about to leave.

The sun was nearly gone. When Berg opened the car door and stood up, looking over the roof of the vehicle toward Ross, Bookman rebundled his overcoat in the cold. Berg stood there watching as Ross searched for and found her keys in the bottom of her bag. It was a Chrysler 300, white—not what he would have expected.

"You're letting in a lot of cold air, fella," Bookman said.

As Ross started her engine, Berg tossed the keys to Bookman and jogged off toward Ross's backing car. Bookman started up the engine and cranked his window down halfway to listen in to the ensuing conversation.

"Nice car," Berg said when Ross stopped and rolled down the window.

"It's a rental," she said, dropping her hands to her lap. "We used it for the trip."

"Oh," Berg said. "I see." He hung his head a little. There was a chemistry between them, Bookman noticed, an intimacy that had not been there just a few minutes before inside the diner. The trip Ross mentioned had been with her new boyfriend. Berg was disappointed with that.

"What car do you normally drive?" Berg asked.

"Oh," Ross said. "Just an old Civic. It's pretty beat up."

"That seems more like you," Berg said. "What color?"

"Green." She asked for no explanation for this seemingly random line of questioning. She too seemed happy to be continuing the conversation, especially sans Bookman. "Is that why you wanted to, you know, stop me?" she finally asked.

"No," Berg said. "It's about *The Secret*."

"*The Secret*? You mean like the book *The Secret*? The movie?"

"Yeah."

"Oh."

"You know," Berg pursued. "How does *The Secret* fit into all this? You mentioned it briefly, but one of the potential suspects is all about *The Secret* and she's not talking at all, which makes her look suspicious."

"You mean that lawyer chick?" Ross said.

"Yeah," Berg confirmed. "Lindsay Enright. You know her?"

"I don't think she did this," Ross said.

"Ok, even so. If you could just humor me a little. How does it fit into all of this, because, you know, I've read it and it seems pretty good, I mean, hopeful, empowering, but it sounds too good to be true."

Ross took a deep breath, let it out. "You can't

judge it with your mind."

"Ok," Berg said.

"You can't think in terms of how it can't be true. You've got to think in terms of how it could possibly be true."

Berg thought about that for a moment. "Ok."

"If this isn't a material world, anything becomes possible." Berg nodded and after a moment, Ross began to sing softly: "'*Row, row, row your boat, gently down the stream. Merrily, merrily, merrily, merrily, life is but a dream.*'"

"What, like *The Matrix*?"

"Like *The Matrix*," Ross confirmed. "Exactly like *The Matrix*."

Berg looked out into space. He was about to ask another question when Ross preempted it. "I'm sorry but this is starting to hit me now, you know. I need to go."

"Sure," Berg said. "I understand."

"But ask your partner there. I'm pretty sure he gets it now."

Berg turned and looked at Bookman, who pretended not to have been listening.

"You'll never be able to apply *The Secret* at this point—no one will. It's like *How to Win Friends* for creative visualization. They can tell you how to do it, but it won't work for you until after the paradigm shift we talked about has taken place. It requires context. It's all about Abundance, right? Tolle provides all the context you need in about a page and a half."

"Where?" Berg shouted at the moving vehicle.

"In a section called 'Abundance,'" Ross shouted

back, eyebrows raised, an ironic lilt to her voice, as if her statement were a question. She shifted to drive and eased away.

"Right," Berg said. "Makes sense."

Berg got in the car and pawed in the back seat for his copies of Tolle's books. He thumbed through the table of contents for *The Power of Now*. Nothing. He found it toward the end of *A New Earth*. It was just a couple of pages long. Berg read it complete in the fading light.

"Hmmp," he said, forehead furrowed, shaking his head.

Bookman didn't bite, stating flatly, "Can we get going now, please?"

"Tolle covers everything in *The Secret* in just a couple of pages. What more context do you need than that? I guess that's what she meant."

Berg put the books down between them in frustration and strapped himself in.

"I don't get it," he said as he backed out of the parking space. "I just don't get it."

Ross was right. Bookman did get it now, but he was in no mood to try to explain it to Berg. And Berg, for his part, knew Bookman had been listening to the conversation and didn't want to ask him again. They drove for a while in silence, until finally Bookman started to feel guilty.

"It all has to do with a school of thought called materialism," he at last relented.

"What do you mean? Like big houses, fancy cars? That sort of thing?"

"No, that would be consumerism," Bookman said as patiently as he could, though the words still managed to escape his lips with a good deal of sarcasm dripping from them. "Materialism concerns the nature of reality. Is what you see what you get? Is what we perceive really real? Does this car have any existence outside of my perception of it?"

"Of course, it does," Berg said. He waited for Bookman to answer. When he didn't, Berg said, "Right? It does doesn't it?"

"I'm not so sure anymore," Bookman said. "If it does, then there's no basis for believing that *The Secret* or religion or anything else of that nature bears any credibility. The two views are simply incompatible."

Berg was a little frightened by his partners admission, in a visceral way he was not at all in touch with. In the hopes of making it all go away, he said, "This has nothing to do with the case though."

"Quite the contrary," Bookman said. "It has everything to do with the case. Drop me off at the cathedral," Bookman said. "I've got a few questions to ask."

"Here's something," Berg said.

> *"Albert Einstein observed, 'The significant problems we face cannot be solved at the same level of thinking we were at when we created them.'*
>
> *"As we look around us and within us and recognize the problems created as we live and interact with the Personality Ethic, we begin to realize that these are deep fundamental problems that cannot be solved on the superficial level on which they were created.*
>
> *"We need a new level, a deeper level of thinking—a paradigm based on the principles that accurately describe the territory of effective human being and interacting—to solve these deep concerns.*

"That's Seven Habits *again," he said.*

"I'm not listening to you," Bookman said.

Chapter 15

On the way to the Cathedral, Bookman's mind had kicked into high gear. In the privacy of his thoughts he could no longer deny, as he had to her face, the irrefutability of what Susan Ross had said. This was a crisis. And the instant she hit him in the solar plexus with Saint Paul's Love Chapter from his first letter to the Corinthians, he knew, in that way of hypothesis formation she and Berg had danced their happy dance over, that Father Justin, his supposed friend since boyhood, had understood this all along.

Bookman didn't know which he wanted to confront more: Justin or a fifth of Old Granddad.

His hip flask was empty.

"Where's Justin?" he said to the secretary who stood guard over the rectory.

She directed him back to the priests' private enclave. And there he sat, longish beard, thin graying hair, gold-rimmed glasses, brow furrowed as he looked up from where he sat to the door where Bookman stood, as if he had been expecting this moment for a while now: What took you so long? read his expression.

They were not alone, but the other priests, old, were just as culpable as Justin was.

"You knew all along, didn't you, Justin?" Bookman said.

"Hello, John," the priest replied. "Good to see you, too. What are you talking about?"

"You know exactly what I'm talking about. I'm talking about Aristotle and Aquinas. You know—all of you know and you're not telling anyone because it isn't in your best interests."

"Now wait just a minute, John," Justin said as the other priests looked at hands and out windows. "Let's just settle down and discuss this."

"It's all clear to me now," Bookman said. "A man named Jesus came along two thousand years ago and preached to the Jews that they were going off in the wrong direction. He spoke to the Pharisees and the Sadducees, two groups of rabbis that had taken on Greek philosophy, each in its own distinct way. At every turn they tried to drag him out on to the field of battle. What was that field of battle, Justin? What is it called?"

"I don't know what you're getting at, John, honestly," Father Justin said, remaining as calm as when Bookman had arrived.

"It's called the dialectic," Bookman said. "Aristotelian dialectic. Argument. Aristotelian syllogisms, Aristotelian logic. Jesus would never go there. He stayed off the battlefield with answers like, 'Render unto Caesar that which is Caesar's and unto God that which is God's.' And 'Man is not made for the Sabbath but the Sabbath for man.' His insight didn't come from the dialectic. It came from somewhere else entirely."

"And where might that have been, John?" Father Justin said.

"It seems like you should know that, Justin," Bookman said. "But for some reason you don't. And then there were the parables. Do you have any idea why he delivered his wisdom in the form of parables?"

"That's easy," Justin said. "Because he had to in order to escape the Jewish authorities of the day. It was a kind of code."

"Sadly, Justin, you're mistaken," Bookman said. "And no one is more familiar with the truth of this matter than I am. I've used it to great effect all my life, both professionally and personally. On the job we collect the evidence, we make deductions, we rule people out and we rule them in. We question people just like Socrates did and we catch them. We catch them when their logic doesn't work out."

"Of course you do, John," Justin said. "That's your job and its an important job. And logic and reasoning can't be overestimated."

"You're right, Justin," Bookman said. "You're right. We do all we can to make it appear that our superiority comes from how smart we are, how much more logical we are. It's all just cause and effect. If you know the cause, you can predict the effect."

"That's right," Justin said.

"No, it isn't right," Bookman said. "And as a man of the cloth you can never believe that it's all cause and effect. The truth is, it's a lie. All those detective novels and the Agatha Christies, the Sherlock Holmeses of the world. It's all one big fabrication. Our reason is not how we solve crimes at all. Something else puts us on the trail and we follow it. We follow it logically but that's not the beginning of the story."

"The hunch," Father Justin said. "The detective's hunch. That's what you're talking about, isn't it?"

"The hunch," Bookman confirmed.

"Well, you're the best in the business, John. Who would know more about the subject than you? If you say it starts with a hunch, I believe you."

"The Pharisees and Sadducees wanted to crush Jesus with their superior rationality. They wanted to prove him wrong. They wanted to drag him out on to the field of dialectic and destroy him in front of his followers. But Jesus knew better than to engage them. He was trying to show them that this sort of mentality was unwise—and wisdom is a concept the dialectic can't digest.

"Jesus spoke in parables because you can't attack the dialectic with dialectic. If you do, its proponents will eat you alive. The only way to attack dialectic itself is through story. Poetry, novels, song, art. The dialectic has no answer for that. Parables are indigestible to the dialectic. If you can't understand them, you can't refute them. Parables are understood with the heart or not at all. Parables and contradictions, that's what Jesus talked about."

"Interesting interpretation," Father Justin said.

"'Blessed are the poor in spirit, for theirs is the kingdom of heaven.' 'But we are great in spirit,' thought the rabbis. 'And surely we will be first in heaven. This doesn't make sense. It doesn't compute.' But the last will be first and the first will be last, Jesus taught.

"The prodigal son, the virgins with their lamps, the faithful and unfaithful servants. They're all about one thing."

"They're all about salvation," Father Justin said.

"Wisdom," Bookman corrected. "They're all about wisdom. What people are calling Enlightenment these days. Salvation is another word for it, but you've perverted that word for your own purposes to the extent that it isn't even recognizable as the same thing anymore."

"Now wait just a minute," Justin said.

"It finally came clear to me," Bookman said. He laughed a little and scratched his head. "You know, I read it a long time ago and something brought it to my mind just now as if I'd read it this morning. Funny how that is, isn't it?" Father Justin didn't laugh. "In Aristotle's Metaphysics, he gives a definition of wisdom right at the beginning of the first chapter. I'm sure you've read it."

Justin nodded.

"He says something like, 'Wisdom is knowledge of certain principles and causes.'"

Father Justin stood up and went to one of the many bookshelves around the room. He pulled out a thick book and opened it to the beginning.

He said, "I think this might be what you're looking for," and he read:

> "Thus it is clear that Wisdom is knowledge of certain principles and causes. Since we are investigating this kind of knowledge, we must consider what these causes and principles are whose knowledge is Wisdom. Perhaps it will be clearer if we take the opinions which we hold about the wise man. We consider first, then, that the wise man knows all things, so far as it is possible, without having knowledge of every one of them individually; next, that the wise man is he who can comprehend difficult things, such as are not easy for human comprehension (for sense-perception, being common to all, is easy, and has nothing to do with Wisdom); and further that in every branch of knowledge a man is wiser in proportion as he is more accurately informed and better able to expound the causes."

"So it's true," Bookman said. "You know. You all know."

"We're very familiar with Aristotle, if that's what you mean," one of the elderly priests said.

"But what he's describing isn't wisdom," Bookman said. "It isn't wisdom at all. It's a definition of wisdom by one who has never known true wisdom. Wisdom isn't 'knowledge of certain principles and causes.' No. 'A man is wiser in proportion as he is more accurately informed'? No. 'The wise man is he who can comprehend difficult things'? No, no, no. This is not wisdom Aristotle is describing at all, is it? Not by our standards. Intellectual, yes. Expert, maybe. Wise man, definitely not."

The priests all looked at Bookman with bovine expressions.

"We have all known very wise people who are not informed at all," Bookman said. The priests nodded in agreement. "Wisdom is something very different from what Aristotle thinks it is. And if you look at his life, you have to believe that though he was a genius, he was completely without the kind of wisdom we're talking about. He was completely unenlightened, as people are calling it these days. He was the precursor of the modern intellectual."

"I'm not sure about that," Justin said.

"Come on, Justin," Bookman said. "The man told Alexander to treat the people he conquered like animals. And he was a pederast."

"Classical Greek pederasty isn't what you think," said the old gray priest who had spoken up earlier.

"And when the Athenians came looking for him,

he was no Socrates," Bookman said. "He high-tailed it out of there."

"Well," said Justin. "Who among us..."

"Aristotle is diametrically opposed to wisdom because he doesn't understand it. Wisdom can't be understood with the mind, it's in a different realm altogether. It comes from direct contact with reality, and therefore with God. From the time he was just a boy, Jesus spoke only of wisdom.

"After his death, Jesus' parables were not understood by the hellenized minds of the early Christians either. Within a couple of centuries, they had turned him into a God, thereby turning his admonitions into the very thing he was preaching against. They equipped themselves to do battle on the Aristotelian plain. They turned God into an idea again, just as the Greeks had done, just as Socrates and Plato and Aristotle had done—precisely what Jesus had told them not to do—and thus a new religion was born."

"You need to be careful what you say," Justin said. "You're running very close to mortal sin and perhaps blasphemy."

"This is exactly what I'm talking about, Justin. You've fallen for Aristotle's worm, hook, line and sinker with all your categories of sins and endless parsing of words and hierarchies of heaven. There's only one sin: unconsciousness of God, and I've never felt more conscious of God in my life than I do right now."

"Good for you," Justin said.

"Once the Christian leaders and their dogma

were sufficiently hellenized, the religion was then co-opted by Constantine—this was just what he was looking for, something to control his hellenized masses. And Constantine further hellenized it. Then came the Dark Ages, so called, and the Church was completely cut off from Aristotle. It seems God was doing everything he could to keep Aristotle away from his flock. But it was to no avail. Aristotle was reintroduced by way of Muslim theologians into Christian monastic circles. Aquinas took his philosophy and made it an official part of Christian thinking, and the Church has been dividing and dying ever since."

An oppressive silence smothered the room. Bookman had said all he had to say. Something in him wished to be proven wrong. He wanted his friend Justin to win this argument but Justin wasn't saying anything. He stood by the bookshelf, Aristotle's open volume in his hand. Resolutely, Justin closed the book and tucked it away in the gap that had been its home for such a long time. He leaned against the waist-high countertop and thrust his hands into the pockets of his black trousers.

"It comes to you when it's too late," Father Justin said. "Once you've been in this business for twenty, thirty years, what else are you going to do?"

"It doesn't add up," Bookman said.

"It doesn't add up," Justin said.

"It's just like you were saying in the confessional that day," Bookman said. "It doesn't stand up to intellectual scrutiny." He wanted to hurt his friend, who had led him astray all these years. He said, "A drunk priest tells the truth."

Just then, a young priest, full of vim, bounded into the room.

"Hello all," he said, smiling, his jet back hair bristling with energy. He felt the tension and said, "What's happening here? Something wrong?"

Bookman opened his mouth to tell him exactly what was going on, as was his way, but Father Justin said, "John, don't. It wouldn't do any good anyway."

Bookman looked squarely at his friend and held his peace. As he left, he heard the young priest saying, "What wouldn't do any good?"

"Check this out, Bookman. It's from Tolle, The Power of Now:

> *"Every addiction arises from an uncon-scious refusal to face and move through your own pain. Every addiction starts with pain and ends with pain. Whatever the substance you are addicted to—alcohol, food, legal or illegal drugs, or a person—you are using something or somebody to cover up your pain. That is why, after the initial euphoria has passed, there is so much unhappiness, so much pain in in-timate relationships. They do not cause pain and unhappiness. They* bring out *the pain and unhappiness that is already in you. Every addiction does that. Every ad-diction reaches a point where it does not work for you anymore, and then you feel the pain more intensely than ever."*

"Why are you reading that to me?" Bookman said. "What are you trying to say, fella? Spell it out for me!"

"Gees, take it easy, Bookman. That's from a sec-tion on relationships. I was talking about myself, the divorce."

"You think I don't already know that!" Bookman said, and he walked out of the office.

"I guess I touched his pain-body," Berg muttered to himself as he turned the page.

Chapter 16

When Bookman got back to the office, he found Berg at his desk and a woman seated across from him, her legs entwined sexily, a leather handbag in her lap. After a moment, Bookman recognized her from the book club meeting at Gack's house. She had been the one to greet them at the door.

"Oh, uh, Bookman," Berg said. "I didn't expect you back this afternoon."

"We have a murder to solve," Bookman said. "Why wouldn't I be back? What's this?"

"Oh, uh, this is Ms. Abercrombie," Berg said. "You remember Detective Bookman, don't you?"

"Delores," the woman said, holding out her hand to Bookman.

"What is this?" Bookman repeated, giving the soft hand a terse grip.

"Oh, uh," Berg said. "I was just interrogating," Berg apologized to the woman with a smile, "Ms. Abercrombie. Just a routine interview."

"A word, Detective Berg," Bookman said.

Berg followed him out to the vending machines.

"Didn't we already interview her?" Bookman said.

"Well, yes, but—"

"And didn't you say that her alibi turned out to be airtight."

"That's the thing about alibis, Bookman, you know that. They start to unravel when you look into them."

"Is that the case with Ms. Abercombie?"

"Well, no, but—"

"What do you intend to interview her about?"

"Well..."

"Isn't her book *Men are From Mars, Women are From Venus*?" Bookman cross-examined.

"So you remember that."

"Yeah, I remember that," Bookman said. "Now you listen to me, Detective, and listen good. A murder investigation is underway and we have no time for this sort of thing. I've got a stack of financial records on my desk that will keep us busy from now until election day all by themselves if you need more to do."

"I just thought—"

"I know what you thought. You thought you'd bring Bambi there down to the station and charm the skirt off her. Not on my watch. Do we understand each other?"

"We may as well hear what she has to say, now that she's here," Berg said.

They went back to their desks. Bookman began leafing through the financial records he'd taken from Sue Ellen Pinkus's house.

"So why don't you tell me about your book," Berg said.

"*Men are from Mars, Women are From Venus?*" Ms. Abercrombie asked.

"That's the one," Berg said.

"Well, first of all, this book really means a lot to me," she said, touching the copy she'd lent to the investigative effort the night Bookman and Berg had come to the book club. "It really changed my life. Before I read it, I would go from one relationship to the next, never understanding why the last one had failed. And of course that's just a recipe for more failure."

"So are you in a relationship now?" Berg asked.

Bookman cleared his throat.

"It's just a routine question," Berg said.

"Not at the moment, no," Abercrombie said.

Berg picked up the book. Because Delores Abercrombie had an airtight alibi, he hadn't bothered to read her book club entry. "Why don't you tell me what you've learned," Berg said.

"First off all," she said, "it really helped me to get in touch with my own feelings as a woman. May I?"

"Of course," Berg said, handing the book to her. When their hands touched in the exchange, they both held them there for a moment before completing the transaction.

"'A woman's self-esteem rises and falls like a wave,'" Abercrombie read. "'When she hits bottom it is a time for emotional housecleaning.' I remember when I read that for the first time. It really hit home with me. It validated all of my feelings and emotions and made me realize it was up to my partner to react to my moods in the right way."

"Hmm," Berg said. "That's interesting. And has this approach worked for you?"

"She said she's not in a relationship," Bookman said. "It must not be working all that well."

"Excuse me for being so blunt," Berg said. "But does this emotional wave have anything to do with your monthly cycle?"

"Of course, it does, silly," Ms. Abercrombie said. "That's the whole point of it. That's what makes us Venetians who we are."

"That's interesting," Berg said. He became lost in his own thoughts.

"What is it?" Abercrombie said.

"Something's kind of coming to me," Berg said. "Something from Eckhart Tolle. Have you read either of his books?"

Abercrombie turned her nose up. "Those are Todd Gack's books. Why don't you ask him about them?"

"Have you ever been romantically involved with Gack?" Bookman asked.

"Oh, no," she said and she shuddered.

"Understandable reaction," Bookman said.

"Here," Berg said. "Tolle is talking about menstruation. This is *The Power of Now*," he said turning the book over. And he read:

> "Often a woman is 'taken over' by the pain-body at that time. It has an extremely powerful energetic charge that can easily pull you into unconscious identification with it. You are then actively possessed by an energy field that occupies your inner space and pretends to be you—but, of course, it is not you at all. It speaks through you, acts through you, thinks through you. It will create negative situations in your life so that it can feed on the energy. It wants more pain in whatever form...It can be vicious and destructive. It is pure pain, past pain— and it is not you."

"Let me see that," Abercrombie said, frowning.

"I remember having to deal with Sally," Berg said. "It was just like that."

Abercrombie, bristling with defensiveness, handed the book back to Berg. "Well, Martians are just as bad," she said. "They're always going into their caves to work out their problems. They're always thinking, thinking, thinking."

"Where is that exactly?" Berg asked. She open-ed *Men are From Mars* again and in a moment, she read:

> "When a man is stressed he will withdraw into the cave of his mind and focus on solving a problem. He generally picks the most urgent problem or the most difficult. He becomes so focused on solving this one problem that he temporarily loses awareness of everything else. Other prob-lems and responsibilities fade into the background.
>
> "At such times, he becomes increasingly distant, forgetful, unresponsive, and pre-occupied in his relationships. For ex-ample, when having a conversation with him at home, it seems as if only 5 percent of his mind is available for the relation-ship while the other 95 percent is still at work.

"And this is what we're supposed to put up with?" Abercrombie said.

"It's your book," Bookman said.

Abercrombie shrugged. With a glum look, she closed the book and gazed disappointedly at its festive lime-green cover.

"So what does this guy—what's his name?" Berg flipped to the cover. "John Gray, Ph.D. What does Dr. Gray say you should do about that?"

"He says you should 'never go into a man's cave or you will be burned by the dragon.'"

"'The dragon,'" Berg repeated.

"The dragon that guards the cave," Abercrombie said. When Berg's expression communicated that he still didn't get it, she said: "If you bother him, he'll be mean."

"Ah," Berg said, momentarily reliving his own marriage. "Yes, well," he said. "He's not being mean, he just wants to be left alone for a while." He picked up another book. "*Don't Sweat the Small Stuff* calls that putting it on the back burner. I guess that's the same concept."

"He's not putting anything on the back burner," Abercrombie steamed. "He's completely preoccupied."

"Yeah, I guess you're right," Berg said. "You know, this is all falling in line with...here." Berg put down *Don't Sweat the Small Stuff* and picked up *The Power of Now*. He found another quote he'd underlined there: "Tolle says, 'As a general rule, the major obstacle for men tends to be the thinking mind, and the major obstacle for women the pain-body.' That's exactly what Grey is talking about."

"This *Men are from Mars* book sounds like little more than a guy trying to tell two A-holes how to get along," Bookman interjected.

Berg looked at Bookman. "Yes!" he said. "That's it. That's exactly it." Berg held out *The Power of Now*. "This Tolle fellow would tell the guy—"

"The Martian," corrected Abercrombie.

"He would tell the Martian to stop thinking altogether, that there are no problems in the present moment, and don't expect people in your life to walk around on eggshells to accommodate your cave time."

"Yes!" Abercrombie exclaimed.

"And he would tell the Venetian to take responsibility for her own inner state rather than expecting people to accommodate her mood swings."

"No!"

"This book," Berg continued, holding up *Men are From Mars*, "is like *How to Win Friends and Influence People* for couples. It's trying to communicate enlightened ideas to unenlightened minds—no offense to you personally, Ms. Abercrombie."

"It takes an Aristotelian approach, as Ms. Ross called it," Bookman said. "Trying to solve the problems of the mind on the level of the mind."

"What's happening here?" Berg said. "We're starting to get this stuff."

"Indeed," Bookman said, a pained expression on his face.

"Susan Ross?" Ms. Abercrombie asked. "Is that who you're talking about?"

"Yes," Berg said. "You know her?"

"I know her," Abercrombie said. "What a frustrating person."

"How so?" Bookman asked.

"I study this stuff every waking moment and can't find a man. She snaps her fingers and three come running to light her cigarette. It's enough to make me want to strangle her sometimes."

"That's what she said," Berg said to Bookman.

"Yes," Bookman said ominously.

"What did she say?" Abercrombie said. "Did you discuss me with Susan Ross?"

"No, not at all," Berg said. "It's something else entirely, about frustration in general terms, Aristotelians versus non-Aristotelians. Tell me, Ms. Abercrombie, what does Dr. Gray say couples need to do to solve these problems?"

"He says they need to write love letters."

"Really," Berg said. "Can you show me?"

"Sure," Delores said. "Here." And she read:

> "Writing out your negative feelings is an excellent way to become aware of how unloving you may sound. With this greater awareness you can adjust your approach. In addition, by writing out your negative emotions their intensity can be released, making room for positive feelings to be felt again."

"Awareness," Bookman said.

"May I take a look at that?" Berg said.

"Of course."

Berg read the passage again and then scanned the next few pages.

"Listen to this," he said to Bookman.

> "Most physical diseases are now widely accepted as being directly related to our unresolved emotional pain. Suppressed emotional pain generally becomes physical pain or sickness and can cause premature death. In addition, most of our destructive compulsions, obsessions, and addictions are expressions of our inner emotional wounds...
>
> "Our society is filled with distractions to assist us in avoiding our pain. Love

letters, however, assist you in looking at your pain, feeling it and then healing it.

"That's the pain-body," Berg said. "That's exactly what Tolle calls the pain-body."

"I still prefer to call it original sin," Bookman said.

"That's exactly what Tolle says you should do for the pain-body, too," Berg said. "Make it conscious. Writing it down is as good a way as any to do that, I guess."

Berg flipped a few more pages and a heading in bold jumped out at him: "'When a man is in a negative state,'" he read, "'treat him like a passing tornado and lie low.' And it seems like his solution to negativity and unconsciousness in others is the same as Tolle's too: non-reaction."

Bookman's phone rang and he picked it up.

"I think we're beginning to catch on to all of this," Berg said.

Bookman nodded uneasily and said, "Bookman...You're working late for a change. What gives?...We'll be right up."

Bookman hung up the phone. "That was forensics," he said. "We may finally have the DNA evidence Farkus is looking for."

"Thanks for coming down," Berg said to Abercrombie. "We'll be in touch."

"I hope so," she said.

"Hey Bookman, check this out:

> *"The cause of our current social crises...is a genetic defect within the nature of reason itself. And until this genetic defect is cleared, the crises will continue. Our current modes of rationality are not moving society forward into a better world. They are taking it further and further from that better world. Since the Renaissance these modes have worked. As long as the need for food, clothing and shelter is dominant they will continue to work. But now that for huge masses of people these needs no longer overwhelm everything else, the whole structure of reason, handed down to us from ancient times, is no longer adequate. It begins to be seen for what it really is...emotionally hollow, esthetically meaningless and spiritually empty. That, today, is where it is at, and will continue to be at for a long time to come."*

"What's that from?"

"Zen and the Art of Motorcycle Maintenance."

"Let me see that," Bookman said, putting on his reading glasses.

Chapter 17

"What have you got, Marla?" Dr. Penny wore a white lab coat, and a pencil stuck from the bun into which her hair was tucked up. She finished stowing a tray of Petri dishes in the glass-fronted refrigerator and took off her glasses before stepping to one of three microscopes lined up on the counter.

"Take a look at this," she said once she'd made

the necessary adjustments.

Berg bent to the eyepiece. "What is it?" he said.

"The wound in your victim's neck was not consistent with a gunshot wound," Dr. Penny said.

"That's why we couldn't find a slug," Berg said.

"Right," Dr. Penny confirmed.

"So what was it?" Bookman asked.

"What you see here is a microscopic filament of a goose feather?" she said.

"A goose feather, huh?" Berg said.

Dr. Penny said, "The kind used in hunting arrows."

"The wound is consistent with a bow and arrow as the murder weapon, then?"

"Yes," said Penny.

Berg thought for a moment. "So what are you suggesting? That the arrow went straight through, including the tail feathers? Or maybe the killer pushed it through after the fact."

"Neither," Dr. Penny said. "There would have been many more feather fragments left behind if that had been the case. I don't know how this one got there. It must have been on the pointy end somehow. It would have been undetectable to the naked eye."

Bookman had gone into a near trance at the mention of bow and arrow. "Let's go," he said to Berg as he left the room.

"Thanks, Doc," Berg said as he followed in Bookman's train.

While they waited for the elevator, Bookman said, "When we were in Kenny Bania's apartment, he had a book called *Introduction to Fletch-*

174

ing beside his computer."

"What's fletching?"

"Fletching is the feathers at the end of a bow and arrow," Bookman said.

"I'll have a black and white pick him up," Berg said.

* * *

"Look, Kenny," Berg said. "We want to go easy on you, we really do." He was sitting next to Bania, straddling the back of a chair. "But you've got to help us out here."

"It's time for you to come clean about Sue Ellen Pinkus's murder," Bookman barked from across the room.

"I already told you," Bania said. "I didn't have anything to do with it."

"We've got the evidence that connects you to crime, Bania," Bookman said.

"It's time for you to tell us about this business plan of yours, Kenny," Berg said.

"How could that possibly—"

"You're our number one suspect, Bania," Bookman shouted, coming across the table. "You're looking at spending the rest of your life in prison and maybe the needle for what you did. Detective Berg, read him his rights."

"All right, all right, all right," Bania said. "A chemical engineer I became acquainted with came up with a new method for the manufacture of arrows."

"As in bows and arrows?" Berg said. "Cowboys and Indians?"

"As in bow hunting and target shooting," Bania

said. "The process made them cheaper and slightly more accurate, though the difference was measurable. It had to do with the alignment of what you would call the feathers. And we were doing it with goose feathers rather than plastic."

"The fletching," Berg said.

"That's right," Bania said. "You've done your homework. The U.S. Olympic Team has shown some interest. All we need now is financing."

"We," Berg repeated. "Who's we?"

Bania's face took on a sullen, constipated look.

"Who's we, Bania?" Bookman repeated.

"I've already told you more than I wanted to," Bania said. "I want to talk to a lawyer."

* * *

"He just lawyered up," Berg said to Chief Farkus.

"I saw that," said the Chief, still facing the two-way mirror. "Now what? We haven't got enough to hold him, fellas."

"He just so happens to be manufacturing the murder weapon," Berg argued.

"Get a search warrant," the Chief said. "You have enough for that. Find the actual murder weapon and we'll talk. Hold him until you turn his house upside down."

* * *

Bookman had been lost in thought as they made their way back to the office. He sat down at Berg's desk and began to pick up one book after the other, picking them up and then putting them down as if the information contained inside were communicating with him through touch osmosis.

"What was it you said to me that day?" he asked.

Berg stood behind Bookman, his hands on his hips. "Which day?"

"You said, 'The ego creates separation, and separation creates suffering.'"

"That's right," Berg said.

"What's that from? Which book?"

"I think it's from *A New Earth*," Berg said.

Bookman picked up the book. "Yes," he said. "Yes. The ego. The ego creates separation. Separation. Differentiation...It wants to establish its claim to uniqueness by differentiating itself from everyone else. It says, 'I am unique. I'm not part of the whole. I'm not part of you.'"

"Something like that," Berg agreed. "All this time I thought you weren't listening."

"That was *my* ego," Bookman said, his mind still masticating, understanding, digging deep, tapping into that great reservoir of knowledge he was just beginning to realize was a part of who he was. He knew who killed Sue Ellen Pinkus—it was all there inside of him—but he didn't know that he knew just yet.

Bookman laughed a little, just one puff of breath, one puff of wonderment. "Could it really be that petty? That picayune?" He hadn't felt this light and free in a long time—maybe not in forever.

Understanding what Bookman was getting at, Berg said, "It could be anything. The ego can even attach itself to something negative, like an illness or complaining. Gossip. Anything."

"It could even be a book," Bookman said.

"Yes," Berg agreed.

Bookman smiled for the first time since the investigation began. This was, in fact, his first real smile in as long as he could remember. It was as if the Universe were calling to him in a way he had not experienced since childhood.

"We already have the one division," Bookman said. "Aristotelian versus non-Aristotelian."

"Right," Berg agreed. "That's how Susan Ross put it." He had already stacked the books the proponents of which were no longer in question in a heap in the corner. Those who's adherents had no alibi were there on the desk. Berg separated them into two piles. In the non-Aristotelian pile, he placed, *A New Earth* and *The Power of Now*—Gack's books.

"All the other Aristotelian books have checked out. *Zen and the Art of Motorcycle Maintenance* was Susan Ross's book. Her boyfriend has vouched for her whereabouts and we have credit card receipts that eliminate her logistically." Berg checked through his notes. "*The Power of Positive Thinking*—well, that was the victim's book."

"Significant for motive," Bookman said. "Some sort of frustration one of these Aristotelians might have felt toward her."

"Right," Berg agreed.

"Then there's *Think and Grow Rich*, Jake Jarmel's book. He and his wife have an airtight alibi. And no real connection there. No motive. And *The Secret*, Lindsay Enright, who also hasn't provided an alibi, but no real connection to Ms. Pinkus other than the book club."

In the other pile were *Don't Sweat the Small Stuff* (the crazy woman at the party, Noreen Young, alibi), *The Seven Habits of Highly Effective People* (Joe Temple, no alibi), *Rich Dad, Poor Dad* (Bania, no alibi) and *How to Win Friends and Influence People* (Romanowski and Genderson, neither had an alibi). All but Young were still in play.

"We haven't narrowed the field much," Berg said.

Bookman pondered for a moment. "No," he said. "That's not it. That was Aristotle's game, endless categorizing, parsing, dividing, and calling that wisdom. No, the universe is trying to point us toward something else. What is it?"

"The universe?" Berg said.

"That's right."

"You're a pod."

"A pod? What's that supposed to mean?"

"You're a pod. You've replaced my partner. What have you done with him?"

"I'm just trying to solve the case, that's all," Bookman said. "If you want to solve the case you've got to get inside the killer's mind. What was the music that was playing in Ms. Pinkus's house at the time of her murder?"

"Let me see," Berg said, turning a page in his notepad. "It was probably, 'I just Called to Say I Love You.' That's what was cued up on the iPod. It was a greatest hits collection by Stevie Wonder."

"Otherwise known as Stevie Morris."

"That's right," Berg said.

"Do you remember reading this Paul Harvey story?" Bookman handed Berg the book, open to the following passage:

> Nature had given Stevie a remarkable pair of ears to compensate for his blind eyes. But this was really the first time Stevie had been shown appreciation for those talented ears. Now, years later, he says that this act of appreciation was the beginning of a new life. You see, from that time on he developed his gift of hearing and went on to become, under the stage name of Stevie Wonder, one of the great pop singers and songwriters of the seventies.

"I remember," Berg said. "I also remember you didn't let me finish reading it."

"Everyone of my generation knows Stevie Wonder's real name. And what did you find littering the interior of Ms. Pinkus's home?"

"Hmm," he said. "I'm not sure." He referred to his notes again and then said, "Money. Bills on the counter, change on the floor."

"Here," Bookman said.

Berg read:

> "Last week I called on a neighborhood grocer and saw that the cash registers he was using at his checkout counters were very old-fashioned. I approached the owner and told him, 'You are literally throwing away pennies every time a customer goes through your line.' With that I threw a handful of pennies on the floor. He quickly became more attentive.

"Yes, I remember that," Berg said.

"Do you recall the stack of magazines beside Ms. Pinkus's sofa?"

"Yes," Berg said. "'Bits and Pieces'? I've never heard of that particular publication."

"Then you don't read very carefully," Bookman said. Here, read this."

Berg read:

> "In an article in Bits and Pieces*, some suggestions are made on how to keep a disagreement from becoming an argument: Welcome the disagreement. Remember the slogan—"

"Etcetera, etcetera," Bookman interrupted.

"Hmm," Berg said, holding the book open in his hands.

"And do you recall that the address stamp had been removed on the magazines?"

"I do," Berg said. "Like in a dentist's office."

"These were not her magazines," Bookman said.

"Who's were they?" Berg asked.

"Do you recall reading this passage to me?" Bookman asked, holding open one of the books.

Berg read it:

> "Eddie Snow, who sponsors our courses in Oakland, California, tells how he became a good customer of a shop because the proprietor got him to say 'yes, yes.' Eddie had become interested in bow hunting and had spent considerable money in purchasing equipment and supplies from a local bow store—"

"That's enough," Bookman said.

"Yes, I remember."

"And this one?"

Berg read:

> "Roy G. Bradley of Sacramento, Californ-
> ia, had the opposite problem. He listened
> as a good prospect for a sales position
> talked himself into a job with Bradley's
> firm, Roy reported:
> Being a small brokerage firm, we had no
> fringe benefits, such as hospitalization,
> medical insurance and pensions."

"Well?"

"That was just a joke about Richard Prior taking up finance," Berg said.

"It was no joke to me," Bookman said. "These
are all from the same book. What are the chances that all of these elements would play a part in
this case simply at random?"

"These are all from *How to Win Friends and
Influence People*," Berg said. "But bow hunting?
And working at a small brokerage firm? All be-
cause of some egoic connection to a book?"

"You said yourself it could be anything," Bookman said. "I'm just stating facts here."

"If your theory holds, that would limit the field
to two."

"Not two," Bookman said. "Only one. Look closer. What do all these passages have in common?
Stevie Wonder; Paul Harvey; Oakland, California;
Sacramento, California; Bits and Pieces; newfangled cash registers?"

"I don't know," Berg said.

"Dale Carnegie wrote the original version of his

book in the 1930s, on the east coast, based on lectures he gave there, in New Jersey and New York."

"These are all from the revision," Berg said.

"And this one," Bookman said, handing Berg the book.

Berg took it and read:

> "Carl Langford, who has been mayor of Orlando, Florida, the home of Disney World, for many years, frequently admonished his staff to allow people to see him, claimed he had an 'open-door' policy; yet the citizens of his community were blocked by secretaries and administrators when they called.
>
> "Finally the mayor found the solution. He removed the door from his office! His aides got the message, and the mayor has had a truly open administration since the day his door was symbolically thrown away.

"Disney World didn't open until when, the 1970s?" Berg said.

"The day we visited Steve Genderson's office, it was in disarray."

"He said he had just moved in and was having it refurbished."

"But the door was off its hinges," Bookman reminded.

"Yes, it was," Berg remembered.

"That door already had his name on it, painted on like it used to be done."

"Old school," Berg said. "And Howbarth and Lowe is an old school, small brokerage firm.

That was Genderson's office all along and Genderson had an open door policy. That's easily verified." Berg made a note of it in his notepad.

"What would be the one thing that distinguishes the people in Gack's book club?"

"They're fanatics about their books."

"Precisely," Bookman said. "And all of them own up to that except for one."

"Steve Genderson."

"On the night of the murder, Genderson came to Sue Ellen Pinkus to show her his latest investment opportunity."

"Kenny Bania's start up," Berg supplied. "Genderson was Bania's partner and when Bania started to get the picture himself, he thought he better think things over and lawyered up."

"Genderson showed her the newfangled arrow, and when she didn't bite, he threw change all over the floor in a last ditch effort to get her attention. When she still refused, he got upset and shot her with the very subject of investment he sought to pitch to her."

"He pitched it to her, all right," Berg said. He looked through his notes. "Oh, boy."

"What is it?"

"Susan Ross is scheduled to meet with Genderson about a business proposition," Berg looked at his watch, "right about now."

"Send out an APB," Bookman said.

"I'm on it."

* * *

When Bookman and Berg arrived at Susan Ross's house, the patrol cars were already on station in front, lights strobing. An EMT van pulled up behind them and Berg goosed the accelerator to get out of its way. He parked in front of the next house and he and Bookman got out and dashed up the lawn.

There was no time for chit-chat as the medical techs took over for the patrolman who was keeping pressure on the wound, near her heart, with a sterile pad.

"She lost a lot of blood," the other uniform said as the techs started a transfusion. "I don't know."

"And the perp?" Bookman asked.

"We didn't get him. The door was locked but, I don't know, we didn't hear anything. We just kind of felt there was something wrong inside, you know what I mean? Both of us."

Berg said, "We know exactly what you mean."

"Just between us, that's not what the report is going to say but it was weird, so..."

"No problem," Berg said.

"We came in and found her laying there. It must have just happened because she would be dead, you know."

"Yeah," Berg said. "Nice work."

"You know who did this?"

"Yeah," Bookman said. "We know. Don't worry. We'll get him."

Just then a call came to Berg's cell phone.

"Berg," he said. "We'll be right there." He hung up. "I think we got our man. He's at Gack's house. He's taken him hostage."

* * *

The sun had gone down behind Gack's home by

the time they arrived. The nearest patrolman had responded to Gack's 911 call within minutes, but by the time he arrived, Genderson had already gotten in and had barricaded himself inside.

"I'm going in," Bookman announced.

"Why don't we wait until the hostage response team arrives," Berg advised.

"Those cowboys?" Bookman said. "All he has is a bow and arrow." He reached inside his overcoat and pulled out his gun and handed it to Berg.

"Are you sure about this?" Berg asked.

Bookman walked up to the front porch and knocked on the door. "Genderson, it's Detective Bookman. Let me in."

"I'll kill him!" Genderson shouted. "I've been wanting to do it for a long time now!"

"Not many will argue with you about that," Bookman shouted back.

"Hey!" Gack ejaculated. "Who's side are you on?"

Bookman tried the doorknob. It turned and he went in.

Inside the great room, where the book club meetings were held, Gack was tied to a chair in the dark. Genderson stood behind him, aiming an industrial-strength arrow, cocked in a compound bow, at Bookman from forty feet.

"Is that thing loaded?" Bookman quipped.

"I was an All-American in archery," Genderson said. "Just missed making the Olympic team. I wouldn't be so glib in your position." Bookman opened his coat slowly to show Genderson the empty holster.

"You can relax," Bookman said. "Susan Ross is going to make it. It's not too late for you, Genderson."

Genderson relaxed the bow.

"I'm not going to candy-coat it," Bookman said. "You're going to do hard time. We know all about what went on at Sue Ellen Pinkus's house that night."

"They're all so smug," Genderson said, his voice cracking. "I work for every contact I make, earn every dollar, and they just fall backwards into both. They hardly ever get mad, and when they do it's over...it's just over."

"That's right," Gack said. "We flap our wings like a duck and swim away."

"Shut up, Gack!" Genderson and Bookman said in unison.

"Me," Genderson said. "I try as hard as I possibly can, but..."

"It's like keeping a lid on a pressure cooker," Bookman provided.

"I know exactly what to do in every situation," Genderson said. "I know that book inside and out. But when it comes down to doing it at any given moment...

"Three marriages. Moving from brokerage house to brokerage house, state to state. I can't keep on like this."

"Jail time doesn't have to be the end of the line," Bookman said. "If you use it right. If your ego cracks and you have the right books."

"This is a case of diminished responsibility," Gack said. "His pain-body did it, not him."

"I'm well aware of the pain-body," Bookman said.

Genderson looked at Bookman and then leaned the bow against the wall. Bookman took out his handcuffs and began reading Genderson his rights.

When the cuffs were in place, he walked Genderson to the door.

"Hey!" Gack said. "What about me!"

* * *

Bookman handed Genderson off to a couple of uniforms.

"Nice work, partner," Berg said.

Chief Farkus arrived in an unmarked Impala and got out of the passenger side.

"What's the status?" he asked Bookman and Berg.

"It's all over," Berg volunteered. "Genderson's on his way to the station."

"Any word on the victim?" Bookman asked.

"Stable, last I heard," Farkus said. "Nice job, you two."

Gack tapped Bookman on the shoulder.

"Gack," Berg said.

"I think an apology is in order," Gack said. "Don't you, Detective Bookman?"

Berg said, "He just may have saved your life, Gack."

But Bookman said, "All right, Gack. I'm sorry."

Gack seemed startled. "Yes, well, apology accepted. It looks like you may have figured out the pain-body, indeed."

"Anything else?" Bookman said.

"No," Gack said, and he started to walk away.
"Yes."

"What?"

"Thanks," Gack said. "For...what you did."

"You're welcome."

Gack seemed suspicious but let it go at that.

"Here, this is from The Secret," Berg said to an unmoved Bookman, "quoting a guy named Beckwith:

> "Creation is always happening. Every time an individual has a thought, or a prolonged chronic way of thinking, they're in the creation process. Something is going to manifest out of those thoughts.

"I gotta tell you, Bookman, I can see how that's true." Berg read it again to himself. "Man, that is so true," he said after a moment.

Chapter 18

The following day, Bookman and Berg visited Susan Ross in the hospital. The patrolman who had administered first aid was already bedside and his posture looked a little too familiar with the patient.

"What's this?" Berg said.

"Detectives," the cop said. "I was just visiting Susan here to follow up with a few questions."

"Susan, huh?" Berg said.

"Ms. Ross," the patrolman corrected.

The detectives didn't otherwise blow his cover story.

"I told you it wouldn't be the cigarettes that killed me," Susan Ross said.

"You're lucky to be here," the policeman said. "If that APB had come a minute later, we wouldn't have been in a position to help you. You've got these two to thank for that."

"Thanks," Ross said. "But I was already seeing

the white light. I had one foot on the escalator. I was curious to take the ride."

"I'm going to get going," the copper said. He was already wrapped around Susan Ross's finger. "I'll check in on you later—to finish my report."

When he was gone, Bookman said, "I've never seen you without a cigarette in your hand. Don't they let you smoke in here?"

"I could if I wanted to," Ross said. Pointing to the IV stand attached by a slender plastic tube to her arm, she said, "I'd just have to wheel this down to the DSA."

"The DSA?" Berg said.

"Designated Smoking Area," Ross provided. "But I've given up cigarettes. I don't enjoy them anymore."

"What, just like that?" Bookman said. "You were on a 5-pack-a-day clip last time we saw you."

Berg added, "Nicotine is more addictive than heroin."

Bookman felt his mouth go dry at the mention of addiction.

"Addiction is an Aristotelian myth," Ross said.

"The pain-body," Bookman said.

Ross smiled. "That's right, detective. Sounds like somebody's been reading his Tolle. I didn't think you paid it much heed."

Bookman, uncomfortable with the affection in Ross's voice, said nothing. His mouth and his throat had turned to dust. His hands began to twitch, one in need of a bottle, the other itching for a glass.

But at the same time, something had clicked inside him. Suddenly, Bookman got something that he didn't get before. Something he couldn't put into words, but he got it. He understood what she meant, he felt it in a way that words could not describe. Epiphany. It was all he could do to remain there in that room, in the hospital. He wanted to get home in the worst way, home to the bottle to see if it was true.

"So how'd you nail Genderson?" Ross asked.

"Turns out he was addicted to his book," Berg said.

There was that word again, addiction. Bookman was getting edgier and edgier. He just wanted to get home but he had one more stop after this one before he could.

Ross smiled a little. "It won't bring Sue Ellen back, but it will give her family some closure. And if we're willing to feel our pain, this will take us all a little deeper. Know what I mean?"

"I think we do," Berg said. "They have you to thank for that closure. We would never have looked in Genderson's direction without your help."

Ross smiled a little again and nodded.

* * *

Father Justin was seated on a bench beside the busy playground. He had taken advantage of the unseasonably warm weather to break out a pair of Bermuda shorts and sandals—his feet and legs had never seen the light of day—though he wore a sweater and windbreaker up top.

"What are you doing here, Justin?" Bookman said, sitting down beside him. "Don't tell me you're one of those priests."

"That's my niece and nephew," he said, pointing to the queue at the foot of the big red plastic slide.

The investigation was over. Bookman took in a deep breath and let it out and tried to bask in the electricity of kids and parents granted a reprieve from cabin fever by the sun. But it was no use, his agitation, triggered beside Susan Ross's hospital bed, hadn't subsided. Indeed, it had only intensified.

"I have just the one vice," the priest said. "And you know what that is."

Father Justin looked at his friend. He noted the signs of an impending binge: Bookman kept licking his lips, kept drying his palms on his pant leg. More than the outward signs, he could feel a certain vibration, one he often felt through the confessional screen when Bookman came around, one that always did its best to worm its way into his side of the booth and into his soul. More than once after taking Bookman's confession, Father Justin had taken deeply to drink in some capacity himself.

"You all right, John?" he said. "Big case cracked. You must be elated. I think you know where that can lead."

"I'll be all right," Bookman said.

Father Justin held up the little book he'd been thumbing through. "The *Tao te Ching*," he said. And he quoted a passage his finger was marking:

> "When the Tao is lost, there is goodness.
> When goodness is lost, there is morality.
> When morality is lost, there is ritual.
> Ritual is the husk of true faith,
> The beginning of chaos.

"Old Lao-tzu kind of called that one, didn't he?" the priest said with a soft smile.

"So where do we go from here?" Bookman said.

"This is where I go," he said, holding up the book again.

"You're becoming a Taoist?"

"A Taoist, and a Buddhist, and a Protestant, and a New Ager, and a Zoroastrian. Wisdom is self-proving; it needs no canon. We will know it when we see it. There's nothing to fear." With a jovial expression, he added, "Heck, I might even check out the Trappists. There's a monastery not too far from here. I think I'll go spend a few days there."

"The Trappists?" Bookman said. "Aren't you taking this a little far?"

Father Justin smiled as he thumbed through a few more pages.

"I'm going to work on it from the inside," he said, turning serious. "I think that's what I'm going to do. What about you, John? What are you going to do?"

Bookman flexed his bandaged hand, just beginning to heal, as he watched the children play. "I don't know what I'm going to do. I feel the urge to let go of everything. I think I might even retire. Move someplace else. I don't think I'm going to be the same person I have been. So it doesn't make sense to live that other person's life."

Justin knew that meant the church too, but he felt no desire to stick up for it, as he might have done in the past.

"I know what you mean," he said. "I'm becoming a different person too. Thanks to you."

"You may not want to thank me," Bookman said. "It feels like complete chaos."

"Instability, yes," Justin said. "Chaos, no. Change is good. It feels good. It feels like it's leading somewhere and I haven't felt that way in a very, very long time."

"Good prices on real estate these days in Florida," Bookman said.

"Good prices everywhere," Justin agreed.

"Something about Florida seems appealing."

"John Bookman in Florida. Who would have thunk it?"

"Yeah," Bookman said. But he couldn't smile. In the ensuing moments, he listened as the voice in his head told him what a great job he had done, how intelligent his cracking of the case had been, how that would rock the sanctimonious Chief Farkus back on his heels for a while.

How he deserved the sweet release a good bender would certainly bring his way.

* * *

As he drove away from the playground (unaware how the conversation had ended, how he had shaken Father Justin's hand, how Father Justin had embraced him in a brief hug, at which Bookman had bristled and stiffened), Bookman once again regained consciousness. He felt the dryness of his mouth, the wetness of his palms, the painful electric tension along his spine on both sides, and he realized for the first time that this was the feeling that had always driven him on. He had always welcomed that feeling as sheer pleasure, the only thing that made him feel alive, that made him feel like himself—who he uniquely was.

But suddenly he realized that this wasn't a pleasant feeling at all. It was unpleasant. It felt like sickness, physical malady.

Yes, that's right, the voice said returning. It was physical malady and the Old Granddad always made it go away.

And that was true, it did make it go away. It was telling him the truth, so maybe he could trust the voice. Maybe Tolle was wrong. Maybe he had it all wrong.

Bookman decided to feel that electric charge in his body, to see what it was all about. He lingered on it, in the cavity of his physical form. Wherever he felt not quite right, he let his awareness hover there feeling the pain, absorbing it without judgment.

He came to one startling conclusion: it wasn't much.

As he pulled his Oldsmobile into a space in his building's parking lot, Bookman heard himself breath these words: "Oh, what little pain controls us."

Inside his apartment, Bookman went to the cupboard that held his lone remaining bottle of whiskey. He looked at the bottle. Held it up to the light from the window over the kitchen sink. The gasoline color of it warmed him.

Bookman cracked the seal on the cap, placed the opening to his lips, tipped back his head. A moment later, he held the bottle up to the light again. A fourth of it was gone.

He felt the heat of the liquid running down his esophagus, the searing pain in his empty stomach—he hadn't felt those sensations in years.

Bookman set the bottle down on the counter and walked back to the door. He took off his trench coat, hung it on the stand, took off his jacket, hung it in the closet, loosened his tie. He sat down in his recliner, pulled the lever for the footrest, leaned all the way back. Waited.

In a few moments, he began to feel the warmth radiating out from his core. He felt his torso relax, his hips, his chest, his arms, his legs.

And just before it reached his head, sending him into sweet repose, Bookman knew that this was the beginning of the end.

"Listen to this, Bookman. Last one, I promise. It's from A New Earth*:*

> *"If in the midst of negativity you are able to realize 'At this moment I am creating suffering for myself' it will be enough to raise you above the limitations of conditioned egoic states and reactions. It will open up infinite possibilities which come to you when there is awareness—other vastly more intelligent ways of dealing with any situation. You will be free to let go of your unhappiness the moment you recognize it as unintelligent. Negativity is not intelligent. It is always of the ego.*

"What do you think of that?"

Bookman pondered it for a moment. "That's true. Very true."

Epilogue

"Things have changed for you, Bookman," Berg said. "I can tell."

Bookman shrugged. "Yes, I guess they have."

"I gotta tell you, partner," Berg said. "I can't pretend to understand everything Susan Ross was telling us that day. Not the way you do."

"I guess it takes a little background to understand it fully. That's the good of an upbringing like mine."

"Care to take a crack at explaining it to me?" Berg said. "I feel like I get it, but..."

Bookman wasn't sure he could put it into words himself, but then he thought about it and he was sure he could, and not just for Berg's benefit. Because he understood it, because of his background, it was incumbent upon him to put it into words and keep putting it into words as long as people were willing to listen. In all his days in the Church, he had never felt this way about any of the dogma around which he'd so dutifully wrapped his soul. This was real. This was helpful. This brought peace and joy—the proof in the proverbial pudding. He was conscious now, and consciousness is necessarily and by definition consciousness of God—of God and nothing else; where did one begin with a stream of words that ended here?

Bookman considered a moment more.

He said, "Everything begins with philosophy. Remember how we were talking about the nature of reality in the car, right after we talked to Ross?"

"I remember," Berg said. "It scared the bejesus out of me, I don't mind telling you now."

"It should scare you in a way," Bookman said. "That's the great philosophical divide. Is this world composed entirely of matter, as Aristotle supposed?"

"Common sense would say yes," Berg offered.

"Common sense would actually suggest the opposite," Bookman countered. The science behind materiality is based on a series of unprovable beliefs, just as religion is. That's what *Zen and the Art of Motorcycle Maintenance* is about. Materialism is a religion, with tenets that people believe in, just like Christianity or Islam. It's the modern mythos that replaced religion. Though that's not what modern intellectuals would have you believe."

"Can you give me an example, Bookman? I mean, science is the opposite of religion, it seems to me."

"You want an example? I'll give you an example. The law of cause and effect. There's an example. This law, so called, is at the heart of the religion of materialism. It supposes that the universe is a cold, neutral place that simply moves about randomly from cause to cause and effect to effect, ad infinitum forever, always has, always will."

"True," Berg agreed uneasily.

"If that's true, what was the first cause? How did all these causes get started?"

"Ah, ha! That's where God comes in, right? God was the first cause. That's how it all comes together."

"But God doesn't exist in materialism. How could he? He isn't made of substance. So in the realm of materialism, this so-called law has already broken down. Materialism can't be true because it can't account for the original cause.

"The closer scientists look into substance, material, matter, the less they find there. The universe is almost completely empty space." Raising his hand, Bookman said, "Your hand, your body, my body. It isn't solid at all. It's more like a frequency, a force field. No substance to it.

"And in the field of quantum physics, when they look at things very closely—experiments— they find subtle differences each time they look, and depending upon who's doing the looking.

This suggests what we non-materialists, we non-Aristotelians already know: that the nature of reality isn't as it appears, but rather is all one thing, something more akin to a shared mind than substance. A shared mind, shared being. That's God and we're part of it, not separate from it. In God we 'live and move and have our being.' That's from the Bible. This is the truth behind books like *The Secret*. It's the only way the law of attraction could possible work.

"But *The Secret* is like *How to Win Friends and Influence People* for creative visualization. It describes how it's done, but you'll never be able to apply it until after transformation has taken place, until enlightenment has been achieved, not to positive effect anyway."

"Interesting," Berg mumbled.

"Let me back track on that a little," Bookman said. "We are visualizing all the time. We are attracting all the time. Look at your own life history and you'll be able to correlate your predominate thoughts, feelings and attitudes with what was actually produced in your life. Everything from becoming a detective to your divorce. You never doubted you would become a detective."

"That's right."

"And you always feared getting divorced."

Berg looked at his feet. "That's right too."

"So did I on both counts. The effects of our visualization is limited only by our ability to seriously visualize an outcome. And that ability becomes unlimited as we fully appreciate the true nature of reality—that it is actually a dream.

"And we're never going to be able to fully grasp the true nature of reality until we awaken to it. Salvation. Enlightenment. That's where Tolle comes in. In his two books, *The Power of Now* and *A New Earth*, he explains step by step what enlightenment is all about. He begins with the nature of mankind in an unenlightened state, that is, a mentality in which the material appearance of the world is confused with the underlying reality.

("Aristotle took this unenlightened state of man and turned it into a philosophy and the modern world has turned it into a religion. Aristotelian metaphysics is merely the codification and exaltation of unconsciousness. That's why in my view, Aristotle is the Anti-Christ, in the broadest sense of the term. But I digress.)

"Tolle talks about the ego and the pain-body. These are the two basic elements of man in his unenlightened state. The ego develops when a person confuses who he or she is with his or her thoughts. When people do that, they process all of reality through this filter, 'through a glass, darkly,' remember?

"I remember, all right," Berg said. "I thought you were going to have a heart attack over that one."

"It was quite an eye opener for me," Bookman said. "This filter is an ability unique to humans in all the universe. But God is not in that mental world of ideas. God is in the real world— God *is* the real world. So those who are trapped in their minds can't sense God and so they quit believing that God exists. Awakening to the real world, where God is, that's enlightenment. Salvation. To put it another way, consciousness is necessarily consciousness of God. But don't get hung up on the words. It's deeper than words."

"At a certain level," Berg said, "that makes sense. But I still don't really get it."

"It's this 'certain level' you're trying to get in touch with," Bookman said. "The goal is to identify your *self* with that certain level, as you call it. The reason you don't 'get it,' as you say, is because you are trying to understand it with your mind. That's never going to happen. Aristotelians would have you believe that rationality is the only way of knowing anything, but as you wisely point out, there is another level of knowing. Get in touch with that and you will 'know the truth and the truth shall set you free.'"

"And how do I do that, Bookman?"

"Seek. That's all anyone can do. Seek. Seek and you will find. Seek with everything you've got and it will come to you."

Berg didn't say anything for a few minutes. They sat in the Crown Vic facing forward. That they didn't have to face each other while discussing these deep truths made both men more comfortable.

"You really have changed, Bookman."

"Yes," Bookman said. "It happened that day in the Chief's office. I fought it. That was ego, too. But once this starts, it can only be delayed, it can't be stopped. Not that you would want to stop it. The incentive is pretty high." Bookman felt himself getting choked up and he bit the inside of his cheek to check himself.

"Are you talking about what I think you're talking about?" Berg asked, thinking of the booze.

Bookman looked at his partner and smiled a little. "What do you say we go get some lunch?"

"All right," Berg agreed, putting the transmission in gear. "Where?"

"O'Grady's," Bookman said.

"Pub food," Berg said. "That's a first."

"There's a reason for that," Bookman said. "I haven't had pub food in a long, long time."

Acknowledgements

I am beholden to my friend Tom Butler-Bowdon for his website www.Butler-Bowdon.com; and his books, *50 Self-Help Classics*, *50 Success Classics*, *50 Spiritual Classics*, *50 Psychology Classics* and *50 Prosperity Classics*. They have been an invaluable resource, spanning the breadth and depth of self-improvement literature.

As an homage, all of the character names have been taken from the most enlightened of all situation comedies, *Seinfeld*, the show about nothing(ness).

This font is Bookman Old Style.

Made in the USA
Charleston, SC
26 October 2011